(A TRUE STORY)

TERREY MCCORMACK

This edition first published in paperback by
Michael Terence Publishing in 2022
www.mtp.agency

ISBN 9781800943445

Michael Terence
Publishing

The Earth is our moving platform from which we observe the motion of the other planets against the backdrop of distant constellations.

CARL SAGAN
COSMOS

Each consciousness is endowed with a creativity of a multi-dimensional nature, so that it will seek to create as many possible realities for itself as it can, using its own significance as a focus to draw into its experience whatever events are possible for it from the universe itself. It will then attract events from the universe, even as its own existence imprints the universe as a separate event with the indelible stamp of its own nature.

JANE ROBERTS
THE NATURE OF THE PSYCHE

To the memory of my father…

CHAPTER ONE

THE GREAT CRAFT listed in the black abyss, as its vast rim angled to the faint light of a near-by star, that glinted on its gigantic rear circumference, making it sparkle like a comet. The enormous forefront, meanwhile, some 30-kilometres further away, edged at a tremendous velocity into silent darkness, as in-flowing multi-matter was minutely monitored on cliff-high 8-dimensional cone-screens within, positioned at the centre of the craft, in Vicinity 20. These screens had displayed consistently how the universe existed in hyperspace-layers of denser holographic reality - something that would be relevant. Indeed, the huge screens were regarded with reverence by the inhabitants, even though other inter-dimensional sentient beings also had similar screens: ideas travelled, it seemed. Luminous vibrations displayed by the cone-screens showed how and where matter oscillated from its holographic source; they also showed in macro-detail energy-concentrations giving illusions of density.

Thus the inhabitants of the great craft *Favola* knew that the universe existed in organised, directed hyperspace-layers - beyond the understanding of their human ancestors in material-level-1, some had surmised during past discussions. Although, that conjecture had disconcerted others, as there were always, some had said, sentient beings who could perceive more than their contemporaries.

Hyperspace-layering was complex. It was where emerging consciousness came from, Favola also knew - but not from whom, or by what. This seemingly magical fact had caused generations on board great perplexity. Plus, many inorganic advanced beings actually dwelled in the layering-horizon almost eternally, as on vast, fixed plains. This too Favola's memory-tanks knew, causing even more mystification - as here, where the great craft was currently exploring a new solar-system.

Designed from exotic alloys to enter and exit black holes, Favola could traverse curvature in its astonishing manipulation of hyperspace. Also dwelling in a type of parallel dimension, it was barely affected by the pull *of* black-holes. Though massive, it danced on the spongy platform of spacetime in a kind of electromagnetic flutter, enabling it to penetrate hyperspace-layering when interstellar.

"New wormholes, I see!" an ancient overseer gasped in the glowing background, as though the very word hurt his mouth. "Offshoots of observed electrons. Ah, fascinating!" A deep-purple light flooded the spacious bridge, as two long wormholes twirled stringily around each other outside. "Dark-energy, as well?" he added, monitoring the bridge's prodigious controls. "Hmm. Interesting..."

Favola engendered the wormholes which it

then shrank to enter. Its mass-location could never be accurately pinpointed because of this, although no structural damage ever transpired. "Behold, tiny anomalies!" the overseer gasped, waving a long arm. The craft took a century to build in lunar orbit, a thousand earth-years ago. It had been travelling since then - a thousand years out from Earth - beyond that spacetime continuum, into alternative parallels within interstellar space, *with a separate Torsion power-source that was almost immeasurable* - used only as propulsion in a given solar-system, as here. Its velocity, though, was precisely calculable, energised via its ten large gravity-amplifiers - though not in digits. Element-115 distorted space in front of the craft via these amplifiers, so in a sense it wasn't velocity. Speed, if it could be called such a thing, was monitored in folding waves of spacetime, as the fabric *of* space became manipulated in front of the craft light-years off - belly-out when interstellar - allowing it to literally fall into the created gap in micro-seconds. Thus, in a flash it could cover many light-years when not using wormholes, allowing the universe to fold back in behind it, sealed, without a trace - as though the universe enfolded itself back into place, Favola had documented.

Alternative human-beings went about their routines, while the craft continued its immortal voyage across galaxies beyond Earth's, into star-sytems which no humans could see, where no humans could be, where no humans would ever know. Then, into the greater reality of intangible, hyperspace-layering within interstellar space, where all living things eventually returned with their life-long payload as individualised conscious energy from any given creature, no matter how small or large. This the screens also documented. Indeed, hyperspace and its inhabitants had always been Favola's destination, though few knew of this seemingly secret mission…

Oddly, many of its inhabitants had never even met each other in the 91 vicinities aboard, for Favola was larger - and more advanced - than anyone living in the 25th century on Earth could have visualized. Its hidden construction, as a consequence during the lifetime of the people who lived back then, became legendary - even mythical. However, by now, in the year 3457 in Favola's almanac, they regarded *Earth* as legendary - almost mythical. For none of them had even seen it, nor had their great-great-grandparents! Because, for them, Favola had no ultimate destination: a return to Earth had never been part of its fantastic plan…

Ergo, human-species were born to dwell within - as Favola was, and could be, their only home. Even though contact had been made with a myriad other intelligent beings along the way, a Favolan's life was inside the vast craft, where the spectacular cone-screens constantly showed a hyperspace-sourced, holographic, molecular-conscious universe, that had mesmerised all over aeons. But where was this source? What made it? What kept it going? These were Favola's deeper missions…

On board, there were huge play-areas within, like the pleasure-domes, which generations had used but not abused. There were metallic streets, float-cars, light-sources, heat-sources, actual Earth-water and soil, plant-life, fish and animals, bionic hospitals, nanotech-repair units, crystal stem-cell clinics, and nutriment-meadows. There were four small forests with rivers and ponds where talks were given, sky-blue Mediterranean-lighting, night-time lighting, and a constant temperature - all used and known by the generations aboard, the people who had, the people who would, live on Favola.

Ergo too, Favola was its own small, unevolving planet - albeit moving at speeds a billion times that of lowly light when required, as silently as clouds on a still day on Earth. Even so, it was easily discernible to every sophisticated alien tracking device that it had skimmed by - and it had graced many over the centuries, monitoring the multi-frequencies of planets itself and making quantum-layered globes of their emerging and lasting realities, which had become one of Favola's lesser missions, via the comically-deranged, speech-impaired, (purposefully, even genetically) amusingly-dogmatic, head-twitching, astronomer-species out on the rim!

"It is our desire to make Favola into its own micro-universe!" one of them had said, on the edges of the craft in Vicinity 91, centuries ago.

This had become a kind of lengthy mantra for them, but the astronomer-species had always been a separate eccentric group of authoritarian misfits - purposefully - and yes, for the benign amusement of everyone else at times.

Not so the Captain, Peeler Curvature, with his short bionic limbs, his nanobotic blood and silver-strewn attire, who stood firmly on the relatively small bridge to the great craft, on square feet, in serious contemplation. For the term 'captain' with regard to something as large as Favola seemed somehow inappropriate - but captain it was, and, at 112 years of age, he was considered as relatively young for such a post, though was possibly the most serious one to date. "Wormholes," he calmly advised, focused. "Move in closer. Hover-plane-8. 10-digit-7." The post of 'captain' did not come easily: the learning-curve was long. His predecessors were normally around 150 before they became captain, and there had been 19 before him. Peeler Curvature was the youngest to date (as well as the shortest) and, as the average life-span for a Favolian was around 500, and captain was a post for life, he presumably had many years remaining as such. And here we meet him, his skills and knowledge regarded as highly admirable. For he once took control of Favola single-handedly, when the craft (for the only time in its history) lost hyperspace-navigational quantum-direction-drive due to an actual clinging space-virus entering one of the computers via a 5-second lag towards a Torsion output: Favola then began heading through the curvature of space into a small sun, on the virus's delinquent request! No human-species had ever piloted Favola before or since, as the dexterity and perception required on the onyx controls was believed to be beyond the potential and understanding of even an officer-species, or, as in Peeler Curvature's case, a navigator-species. (Both could attain the post of captain). It was to Peeler Curvature's mythical credit, therefore, that he had done so, saving the great craft, while bypassing the computers *and* Corda, of whom more in a moment. Atomic-scale-blocking was then invented to prevent any future viruses from entering, which was when Favola became a wholly sterile environment…

"Sharp. 15. Lower-plain-4. Level. 29. Ease to angle. Sharp… 12. Yes. Good." His confident commands resounded throughout the humming deck, as he stood hyper-focused before the large ocean-like viewing-platform at Favola's forefront. The craft was being navigated close to the orbit of an emerging planet, via the Torsion drive - a world that had itself several frequency-rings around it, which, to them, also denoted that it existed more firmly in other, perhaps lighter frequencies, simultaneously. This was fairly common, as Favola knew. The forming orb had only recently been discovered by the astronomer-species, and there was also a large sun in the blackness that had a spinning neutron star as a twin. This twin had also only been visible to them for some 2 Earth-years out - minutes aboard Favola. So, slowing the vast circular craft down from its space-enfolding phenomenon, (subsequently coming out of hyperspace in a flash on entering this solar-system) Peeler Curvature was being observed carrying out his ancient traditions on the bridge by the kindly overseer-species, always clothed in gold. "Sharp. 14. Medium-plain-11. Level. 28." His calm commands resounded.

"Ah, emerging spheres beyond!" gasped an overseer - one of three.

"This is what Favola had speculated," suggested the captain.

"Yes, but to actually see them! Miraculous!"

There were many human-species living on Favola, of which the overseer-species tended to be the oldest, and were *not* overseen themselves. Life aboard Favola had not evolved as life had done back on Earth. Earth - with its domed landscapes, its biosphere cities, its undersea villages, its green and built-upon poles, its vast underground ancient cities, its portable towns, its alien neighbours - its firmly monitored inhabitants? Life aboard Favola had more or less remained how it was at its launch. For no 'culture' as such had been inherited - except, perhaps, a kind of stale English language via a number of old texts. While on Earth it had raced on and through a thousand earth-years of hyper-technology that was now largely at submicroscopic robotic levels, which were fully in control of everything, including, when rarely required, justice. The fabulous technology, though, gave birth to previously unimaginable probabilities for the humans alive who towed the firm line, monitored as they were, though the lack of ancient freedoms made this fact seemingly irrelevant to them. Therefore the two, Favola and Earth, were of course very alien to each other by now. For only a handful of still semi-functioning antique *robots* on Earth, in a remote community, knew of Favola's existence out in deepest space through the uploading of human brains many centuries ago - though no contact could be made. As mentioned, the citizens of Favola had never seen Earth - except for one. Consequently, Favola was now a time-frozen, unique microcosm of how Earth had been back in the 25th Century!

"Captain, the rings are in view. Observe." The android at the helm, the only one aboard, was called Corda (pronounced with a smooth 'r'). Corda had existed for as long as Favola, and was designed *for* the craft and to exist *within it* - for all time. At 2.2-metres tall, though ultra-lean for the height, Corda was actually genderless, *yet immortal!* It had no working parts that could wear out, and only Corda had the total capacity to control Favola's trajectories, especially in the strangeness of the folding of hyperspace. Corda also ran the old on-board 28th-generation quantum computers, which were occasionally updated by software that was often being invented by the scientist-species.

Corda could connect into new software should any problems arise - which was rare. For Favola itself was almost a self-repairing, organic entity. It communicated with Corda via submicro-computers in a type of short-hand which no human-species understood, as was the plan. Yes, Favola almost lived! If problems *did* arise, however, Corda - the only one aboard to have seen human-species other than those on the ship - would be on it immediately. The maintenance-species would then be informed of what was required, and would act, with Corda directing them, who, in a way, was a kind of angel to all aboard. Born, as it were, inside Favola, the texture and colour of its skin-covering often matched that of the shades and nuances of the bridge, also notating moods or emotions almost musically. (Emotions were known to engender new electromagnetic units in people, which would become tangible objects within the vast arena of hyperspace, and Favola monitored this). Under normal conditions, however, Corda had a grey tinge of yellow combined with a hint of green - shades often depending on the galaxy they were in, or of objects created mentally by all aboard, which often surrounded the craft. It was a complex concept by 25th-century standards - though not now. By now, Favola would have been regarded as wholly ancient to human-beings on Earth in the 35th-Century.

"Thank you, Corda. Angle. 13. Sharp. 40."

Peeler Curvature stepped closer to the huge trans-core viewing-screen, which could survive the implosion of a star. He stood on the viewing-platform, angling his head while faintly frowning. The rings to the planet were now visible below the massive craft, but what could also be observed on the planet's surface were tiny lights going on and off, as though explosions were taking place. However, explosions were not currently being monitored by Favola. "Corda, the flashing lights? What are they? What takes place?"

Corda instantly translated Favola's short-hand. "Sir, Favola informs me that space-fissures appear to be transpiring in the unstable structure of the planet's emerging rock-structure. It is most unusual. Favola has rarely encountered such a phenomenon before in the formation of a planet. There is also a great heat being generated, registering 10 trillion K! Subatomic particles are now active."

Favola had shown that planets actually emerged from hyperspace, and were not formed long-term by gravity simply fusing dust-particles together. This might seem strange to 25th Century people, before it was demonstrated by quantum-imagery. "It is…" gasped the captain, "resplendent!" He gazed down at the amazing surface below them, balancing as he bent forward to allow the telescopic lens in his bionic eye to focus. Some activity on the bridge then as others wished to observe, including the two elder - and somewhat mysterious - long-limbed overseer-species in their golden gowns. This activity slightly disconcerted Captain Curvature, whose title no one even blinked at. (It was true that sarcasm or irony had never existed on Favola, and perhaps never would). "Fissures in time?" he whispered, mildly perplexed. "Most... unusual. Myriad consciousnesses arising!" He was even jostled a little, easing a crew member out of his line of vision, respectfully.

"Sir, Favola informs me that the amount of emerging conscious-units are affecting the planet's structure, filtering out denser frequencies. There could be danger for us." Corda's genderless voice-tones remained calm in their warning, though its colour did alter slightly to a pinkish brown. Powerful green lights flashed into the bridge from the planet below, forming electric rainbows within.

"Miraculous!" the overseer-species gasped again, holding out his long hands.

"We will need further structural tests," Curvature then logically commanded. "I want a chosen team to go down to the surface in Alternate-craft 6. Once the structural tests indicate that there might be a safe but brief slot, our search will continue. We will commence work. Emerging orbs are where our objective is, as we know. Corda, 18. Angle. 21. Flat. Level. 9 - across 7!"

A pause. "Sir, Favola informs me that that gradient could be dangerous. It states that our current angle would give us a greater chance of entering hyperspace should the planet implode, which, Favola informs me, is likely to happen! There is also a stellar-mass black-hole less than a light-year from our present location. This could have a bearing on our swift escape."

"Corda, I have given a command. I know that Favola airs on the side of caution at all times, especially with emerging units thus, but I sense no danger is imminent. Now then, angle. 21. Flat. Level. 9 - across 7!" Peeler Curvature patiently waited for a response from Corda…

Who frowned very mildly, then tilted its head. The pinkish-brown shade on its skin-covering deepened. Favola then informed Corda personally that it was going to angle 21, as the captain had ordered, even though it feared for it and the population's safety, but that it would confidentially place a contingency coordinate in case of danger. At angle 21, Corda continued to frown as though expecting something to happen - and it did. For at angle 21, without warning, the spacecraft was instantly transported to another location in the universe - another galaxy altogether - in a flash too quickly for even Favola to act independently! No structural expansion had taken place, yet in the space of a nano-second they were some 70 thousand light-years from their original position - Torsion-drive ticking over, inactive. Favola instantly located their new setting, and reported it to Corda, who then calmly said, (while returning to its original colouring) "Sir, Favola informs me that we have been conveyed to a new location in the universe, and even..." Corda paused thoughtfully to fully take this information on board... "a different fabric of spacetime! We have shifted in time, sir - backwards! Alas, you were mistaken, captain. We *were* in danger..."

Peeler Curvature and others looked to Corda for more of an explanation, but none came. The captain then asked for clarification from his first in command, and, for the first time in a generation, a seemingly evolving Favola actually spoke through Corda, in tones distinctly wistful, if not somewhat distant, but clearly female in their wind-like transmutation. "We are... now part... of moving frequencies in a spacious present. They move in the universe holographically, but in continuous circles. They have transported us... within the present, to more than a thousand years into the circular past, *of* the spacious present. This is the universe... of a thousand years ago!" Favola then, after a brief silence, began taking readings and soundings of the new location...

...The two overseer-species on board the bridge gasped at the stars outside, and went to kneel. This sudden and unexpected (if not abstracted) direct communication with Favola caused them to almost panic. The captain calmed them through gestures, then walked over to Corda, who appeared tranced. He stood next to it, observing the glass-onyx instruments at its finger-tips, and saw that, yes, they were certainly not at the planet's location anymore, and that yes, Favola's voice (if indeed that's what it was) was coming from Corda's inert mouth. The captain looked more closely for movement, but there wasn't any. Instead, Corda then came to with a mild jolt, and looked *to* the captain, who glanced back at the instrumentation with some perplexity. "Corda, what goes on? I sensed no danger."

"Sir, I believe that Favola has just spoken through me. I am vaguely programmed to allow this, though it has only ever happened once before. Favola's concern was very profound, as stated. You were warned about going to a closer angle to the planet. This was why *she*… has now communicated."

"She, Corda?"

"Yes, sir. Favola has been evolving. She is now… female!" Corda then blinked heavily and twitched a little at this curious declaration. A new sensation entered the inert electrolyte fluid that conducted Corda's brain-patterns, enabling thought and the holding of a unique, broad consciousness. For two seconds it entered a new philosophical debate with him/herself, concerning gender.

"Corda, that is impossible!" one of the overseer-species quietly commented from the glowing background. "I too sensed no danger at the planet. Plus, there is no one aboard who has heard Favola speak. Favola is our world, not a female talking craft! Nor is it a living entity. No. It cannot be!" He waved a long arm.

"Quite, sir. But it appears so. And for me, too. I have just discovered this for myself." Corda turned to look at the overseer. "I am also having some difficulty with the idea, sir. Favola has spoken through me before, but that was 800 years ago and sounded robotic. She is now conscious of herself!"

The captain then demanded that, "We have more pressing concerns presently. If we've gone back in time a thousand years in an instant, then it could only be some sort of particle-smashing electron-shoot from that imploding planet! My sincere apologies if I have misjudged. It seems that we have perhaps been shot from the imploding planet, electromagnetically through the holofield, I would suggest, via its star, like a pointlike particle. Can we calculate what our velocity might have been? My only hope now is that we have not interacted with ourself on the other side of this time-fabric, and mutated into anti-matter! Our Element-115 should prevent this, however, even though it can also create it, as we know. But, it may not have had time…"

"We can calculate wave-speed-probability," one of the scientist-species helpfully suggested. "But why do we need to know this, captain'? It must have been at least 10-trillion times the speed of light!" He seemed as baffled as everybody else.

Corda then solemnly turned to the captain and declared that: "All motion-drives are at a standstill, sir. We are at an unknown location in spacetime. I await your instructions…"

CHAPTER TWO

IN THE AWESOME ARENA of Vicinity 20, which was positioned directly at the centre of Favola, monitoring the cliff-high 8-dimensional cone-screens that had miraculously recorded in one crumpling moment the inflowing dark-matter from a thousand years from Favola's last known location to this present unknown time-flung one, Peeler Curvature watched with intense intelligence a higher-dimensional warping of magnetically altering strangeness that stood and distorted in an electrical visual fireforce some 50-metres tall in front of him. As well as it being all around him, surrounding him in a supervirtual sense, it was a time-squeeze in a 28-dimensional water-sculpt!

Strange noises and wonderful sights abounded in the harmless great space, that simultaneously became submicroscopic *and* gigantic, as the word *transported* then entered Curvature's mind…

Time, by Favola standards, did not exist, as it had done on Earth. Time aboard Favola, as it often travelled beyond light-speed, into and through the quantum singularity of black holes which went *beyond* time's bendy fabric, as well as dwelling in this parallel dimension to the universe (not to mention hyperspace-travel, which no one on Earth had fully understood until this exotic alloy created it for itself), was perceived extremely slowly, or, most often, not at all. Well, except when reckoned by someone approaching their 300th birthday, say (even though a year was not a year on Favola, it was a hundred-times more by Earth-standards). Or, at a critically low velocity in orbit around a planet, where *time* suddenly began to have a heavy effect on things. No. Time had almost zero effect on the human-species aboard. This made them 3-dimensional - as they all knew of time, as, indeed, they all *knew* of the Earth - but 7-dimensional in the sense that they were removed from the basic laws of the universe where big physical entities needed to subsist in a solar-based gravitational 3-square environment. They weren't covered in time, as it were. This meant that in reality - that is, Earth-time reality - Favola had been away from its mythical origins for some 100,000 years, and that, by Earth standards, each inhabitant actually lived to be about 60,000!

Peeler Curvature (navigator-species) watched visible quantum-information crumple the fabric *of* spacetime - a fabric which it created. Supernovas created atoms, which were nothing but holographic reflections from their own electrons; but Favola knew that dark-matter created the *actual hologram-fabric* of spacetime! This could be seen in Vicinity 20. It rippled all around, with dark-matter also engendering neutrinos, which made an exotic electricity that had a superposition-type magnetism to it which Peeler Curvature could also feel, in its different dimension. This then danced and twisted, as it brought simultaneous bubble-spheres into being. The captain knew that it didn't normally twist in this manner, however. Without being aware of how long he watched it for, or of what else needed watching *as* he watched it, what he saw seemed to give light on the fundamental string-holograms of the universe. It was… *older* dark-matter, it seemed to him. Older, yet newer.

Reading all this as though having the language to understanding it, ideas were placed in his head, which, he vaguely felt, hadn't been there before. These ideas could, he speculated, illuminate their time-flung plight. For there it all was, squeezed in from a thousand years in one single moment! He stood watching the cone-screens twist and weave as he'd… never seen them do before. Exotic particles as though from an atom-smasher were generated in front of him. And there, some 15-kilometres away from the bridge, with its cavernous hugeness echoing to clicks and hums and bangs and lightening crashes, (un-felt heat, speed-twists, 15-dimensional liquid-bulges, the weak-force of un-felt gravity rising, an image of melt-down radiation with fire) these recorded shapes and movements made actual sensations that would have terrified a 21st or 22nd century person to death. Literally. And to be alone with these shapes in a massive spacecraft that was inert at a distant unknown location in the universe, (or the Metaverse?) in a chamber the size of a cathedral, without having grown up amongst it, so to speak, would have no doubt hypnotized an earlier person in a frozen, terrorized, blood-curdling trance! For it was the actual vision of the universe evolving and transforming in the higher dimensions that it *did* evolve in - holographically. It was all on display!

The captain, though, didn't flinch. Fear played no part in his psyche. Besides, it was far too interesting to be afraid. There was nothing *to* fear!

But then somebody spoke in his head. "Hello? Yes?" Silence followed this into his ear-implant. "Who is it? This is the captain. Speak please."

Peeler Curvature tapped his ear, then went on scanning what was before him. The cone-screens, in a sense, were as reassuring to him as perhaps the pyramids were to the ancient Egyptians on Earth. They were part of the scenery, part of life, part of everyone's psyche - aboard Favola. These ten great oval screens connecting up as one, positioned strategically in the vast vicinity, were known to all and used by all. *They were the pyramids of Favola!*

A tapping re-echoed in his head.

"Sir, you are required back on the bridge," said Corda's voice softly in Curvature's ear-implant amid the external sounds. Voices in the head. That's literally what most inhabitants of Favola had while on duty: *voices in their heads of other crew members via ear-implants.* Corda mostly, who could directly communicate with every single human-species aboard (many at the same time) at the press of a thought-button, as now with the captain…

"Understood. I'll be on my way. Inform me as I go, Corda." For it had seemed to Corda that Favola, which had subsequently been placed back at the imploding planet and the original time-fabric, had not moved at all.

The velocity could not be calculated, his report would say, as it never transpired.

Therefore, the overseers would conclude, the captain was correct not to be concerned about going to the angle which Favola advised against, as Favola had not been time-flung at all, in a sense. There was, they would say, no real present danger, and he acted admirably.

Corda was now preparing for an emergency: the ultra-geometric navigation of a hyperspace-leap. He/she was making the decision with Favola herself - communicating with various required human-species via *their* ear-implants, concerning certain trajectories. Its eyes widened and its face and head remained completely inert (turning to grey) as it prepared to literally steer the great craft from finger-touch controls and a light-jump scanning brain combined with a quasi-subatomic multi-dimensional thought wave-pattern that would then verbally communicate with other human-species the more simpler required instructions - mostly about motion-drive monitoring. But the captain traditionally needed to be there whenever light-speed was attained, (even emergency light-speed) though he couldn't calculate himself in more than 6-dimensions. An initial backup was required in case something went wrong - which rarely happened. Indeed, every captain of Favola had skills in light-speed handling - if required for a brief period. And *handling* it was still called; although Peeler Curvature had been the only one to have ever actually done such a thing - when it had been required, as mentioned.

He left behind 10-to-30-dimensional shapes, via 8-dimensional cone-screens, as unusual sounds resounded in Vicinity 20 from a sound-system that was the very best Earth had to offer in 2457. For if light was known to a 25th century child as photon-vibrations creating the fifth dimension, then the size-picture of the universe created by a multi-dimensional explanation of dark-matter's quantum mutation all around it was *sound.* Deep sound. With a thousand years of these metamorphic distortions of geometry packed into one long quantum moment, a twisting Vicinity 20 held the captain's interested absence - even when it was, well, absent, which itself remained, interested still - even as he himself floated to the bridge on his own personal float-car on one of the many highway-tracks. This would take him about 30-minutes - had time existed. It was a pleasant trip, though.

It lengthened. It bent. It swelled. It rose. It contorted. Then it drew liquid breath. Peeler Curvature's image became part of ancient dark-matter's governing machinery and mechanics -

albeit outside the realm of 25th century human perception…

Light was known to humans in the 25th century as the fifth dimension, after time - the fourth, and curled-up space - the sixth. Humans in the 25th century lived in six dimensions, and *dark* would be known to future generations as dimensions 7-to-30, the overseers would one day conclude! Darkness augmented everything beyond six dimensions - including the five beyond the next five, and so on. For darkness ruled in the universe, the inhabitants of Favola would discover. Darkness governed the universe like a god. But darkness became light when the viewing was done by a 10-dimensional creature, who could simply walk through walls and not even be seen. Yes, superior beings abounded in the cosmos - 'superior' being subjective to a 6-dimensional creature, naturally. They were all around. 10-dimensional creatures subsisted in the 6-dimensional known universe, while still existing in their own sphere(s). 10-dimensional beings made up the vast population *of* the universe - albeit in parallel ones, simultaneously. We just didn't know about them.

Well, the inhabitants of Favola didn't - but that would change.

It was a 10-dimensional being who spoke through Corda's mouth, via Favola herself - but that hadn't been made clear as yet, even to Corda. Although Peeler Curvature, as he floated casually back to the bridge in relative luxury and absolute safety, while bypassing his favourite pleasure-dome, had a strange inkling of something like this. Of something of this nature. For as Favola's fresh air streamlined through his longish hair; and down a longish, fairly busy avenue he went under a sky-blue ceiling; the captain had a sense of being observed. It wasn't simply his own ego watching him. It was something much more tangible, if not more benign and loving. It was something more incredible, too, not earthbound, as it were. What Peeler Curvature sensed was something more miraculous than any infantile superstition. *Transportation!* was the word which came to mind.

The captain's favourite pleasure-dome illuminated his face from its neon fantasy, as he then vanished into the Favolan night towards the bridge, (which was already in darkness). He allowed himself a wry smile for the first time in a while, thinking briefly of his last blissful trip there, and how many pulsar-credits he'd spent in pleasure's elusive but electronic pursuit. A lot, was his puzzled conclusion…

Ethereal 10-dimensional beings observed his perplexity without mystery.

Favola had a cycle of mechanized night and day. Vicinity 20 was currently at dusk, as Peeler Curvature headed into the night-time cycle at the front-end of the great world. At the front-end of the great craft, as he entered night fully; a subtle night-lighting taking over from a wispy daylighting; it struck him again that he was being watched. So much so that he needed to actually turn his head from the programmed vehicle to look behind. Nothing. Just the road and one or two other float-cars going the other way. This gave him more puzzlement, which, as an enigma, puzzled him even more.

The bridge was a hive of activity.

On entering, a number of officers gave the Favolan salute to the captain, who simply nodded in return in the given tradition. He was then seated on the right hand side of Corda, who had been tranced while calculating their trajectory. However, Peeler Curvature had not given the command for hyperspace; it was Corda's design. (Was Corda in control?) He needed to know more straight away. "Corda, desist! Officer Fabritius, desist! We remain!" Curvature then placed his hand on Corda's heated one, and Corda came out of his pre light-speed hypnotic state, turning a pale green.

"Sir," he then whispered, "I understand your concern, but if we do not vanish from this location we maybe time-flung to somewhere where we might not return! It is imperative that-"

"Corda, when Favola spoke through you, tell me about it. Tell me how it felt - how it seemed. I think that perhaps it was not Favola…" The captain looked at him intently.

Corda returned the look with atypical consternation. The captain's reasoning seemed most abstract. "How… it… felt, Sir? I do not understand."

"Something more happened to us than a time-fling, Corda. In Vicinity 20 I had a widening sense that I was being perceived by something from a higher level of reality in our holographic universe - perhaps from a level higher than 7. Some ultra-dimensional gazing took place. That's the only way I can describe it. What I gleaned was that beings from other dimensions - remember how we almost encountered them in the 116 solar-system in galaxy M409, but they eluded us? Beings from other dimensions spoke through you, Corda, telling you to take the ship to where they wanted it to go! I cannot prove this. I have no scientific evidence: I am acting on intuition."

"Sir, are you feeling okay? You look a little pale…"

At that moment the planet began creating larger explosions on its surface, causing mild shock-waves to be detected by Favola in its upper-atmosphere. The captain's attention was taken with this. "Officer Fabritius, Angle. 30. Curve to swerve. 49. Sharp. Hover-stem 84!"

The officer acted quickly. Favola's vastness moved without sensation to the captain's new command, who used his telescopic lens to further his reading of what transpired. And the other officer-species too, as they also had telescopic lenses implanted as children, came forward to help in the reading. They used themselves in a kind of synchronized scanning motion from the viewing-platform, all under the watchful eyes of the two overseer-species, who themselves simultaneously observed what was taking place. The planet was seemingly getting ready to time-fling Favola once more. It seemed likely. And it did. In a flash.

While it was true that back on Earth, wherever Earth was, the date was actually 3457, Favola's distances had placed it way into the future, and so dictating *time* and *dates* was impossible. The further it got from Earth (via hyperspace) the more into the future it travelled, so to speak. And it was also true that the inhabitants of the craft lived to be, as they perceived it, about 500, and that Favola was a thousand years old. But a thousand years out from Earth at even light-speed, would, had the craft then returned, been more likely to be one-hundred-thousand years. So, Favola's inhabitants, as has been said, were literally around for thousands of Earth-years as living creatures, (outside of time really) witnessing things that no Earthling would ever see. Even Corda couldn't actually *know* how many years may have passed on Earth in their absence from it - to say nothing of what might have transpired there. If one minute at light-speed equalled a passing decade *on* Earth, as it did, then what would the date be while travelling for many years at more than the speed of light, and then time-flung by immense and exotic magnetism?

And so it was that Favola, from this second time-fling, in all its might and size, found itself in orbit around a blue planet - its disk-shape in the sky looking like a full moon to the inhabitants *of* that planet way down below on its glass-gleam surface…

CHAPTER THREE

AT THE TIME of Favola's departure from all known human things, the invention of The Transdoor - an offshoot of Favolian technology, was taking place on Earth. The Transdoor combined atomic heat-flash engineering, which was engendered from the exotic matter known as *Nebstron,* that Favola used in its manipulation of hyperspace. It was just that: a movable door containing a large metal plate, that led into a metre-long negative-energy passageway (where the Nebstron instantly de-materialized your molecules) which then led to another door containing the same sized metal plate, which, in turn, opened out onto any destination on the planet - so long as the destination itself had a Transdoor that could connect the voided passageway to collect your re-materialized molecules. (Like a wormhole, but not a wormhole). It aligned itself perfectly parallel to *your* door through advanced geometry. It was difficult to get right at first, but that was only because of the geometry and the special angling of each door to each distant contact…

One punched the coordinates (heat-flash-digits) into your own panel in your abode, stepped in, closed your door, stepped out into an apartment in New York, say, or a hotel in old Chicago, or a lakeside bubble-dome. Anywhere. Transdoors were eventually fitted to every abode and building on the globe - including the undersea villages *and* the settlements on the moon. It was becoming the main mode of transport by the year following Favola's launch: Earth-time, 2458. Particle-shifters. Even parcel-shifters. Transdoor was totally revolutionary!

This was a clue as to the period, as well as the planet, that Favola now gently orbited: a female scientist from California who had been perfecting the project, along with her two children, accidentally stepped out onto Favola's spectacular bridge in a flash of light, turning Corda yellow. Yes, Earth, by the time of Favola's launch into deep space, was just becoming a Type I civilization, in that it was now acting as a planetary civilization, and could control the energy-resources of the entire planet. It could harvest the oceans, prevent earthquakes and other natural disasters and could mine deeper into the planet's crust than it had ever done before. (A Type II civilization, out of interest, and by contrast to this, was one that, still by then a thousand years off Earth's technology, could use the energy and power of its star for its own needs - actually mining its very sun - thereby easing the strain on its planet's limited resources by powering its machines with limitless direct solar energy. It would have already been subsisting as a planetary society for many centuries. A type III civilization, by contrast again, had the capacity to harness every star's energy in its galaxy simultaneously, thereby providing a power that could enable it to enter the 10th dimension via the Planck length, which was a distance so small that it required immense energies to probe into it, from which, paradoxically, immense distances could be achieved, as well as time-travel. Type III civilizations were everywhere in the cosmos, including the galaxy that Earth was in. Type III civilizations were usually 10-dimensional beings. Like Favola itself, they existed in *imaginary time)*.

At first the woman thought she'd reached her brother's place on the moon, who was living and working there as an engineer to one of the mineral mines. She frowned when she saw Peeler Curvature, then held her mouth when she saw Corda, who genteelly stood (such height!) as if to welcome her. It was never understood how her Transdoor-readings directed her material to the bridge of Favola, (it may simply have been the exact line of trajectory, of Favola itself creating a weird anomaly in the fabric of spacetime by being where it shouldn't have been - by being in imaginary time made real). For no one at that period had been transported to anywhere that did not have another door. There had been no accidents to date. However, being from the mid 25th century, she could only have guessed at the technology she beheld: it had never been used on Earth, as such. It possibly exceeded the capabilities of a human mind to comprehend! The coloured glass, (was it glass?) the oblique contours, (were they contours?) the blue metal (was it metal? was it blue?) Then her children began to whimper a little in a kind of fear, and she began backing away towards a transparent panel (was it a panel?) that was being monitored by an officer, and which could be walked through, who himself began backing away from that. Squinting at the vision, to him this person looked like a Portrait of Dora Maar by Picasso, in that, living in an extra dimension as such, he somehow viewed every angle of her face simultaneously. It was fascinating, yes, but daunting as well. Such features! For she had longish dark hair which he'd never seen before, and startlingly big eyes, which also viewed him, as an alien! Each was alien to the other!

The human-species aboard Favola had been bred and even designed to subsist only there. At the time of its launch they did not exist on Earth, (the whole project was kept a conspiratorial secret) except for the overseer-species, who were descended from the defunct religious people. (To digress, by the mid 25th century on Earth it was commonly acknowledged that consciousness formed the brain, which was proved to be an actual event-forming psycho-mechanism through which the consciousness of every single creature operated. A staggering concept to earlier people, but fully accepted by later ones. There was no 'creator' as such, so all religions were systematically fazed out along with the controlling but fading dynasties, who had been giving politicians the orders all along, it transpired, and so the fakery of politics, too, was eventually discarded. Freed-up scientists were then allowed to show that consciousness survived the demise of the brain that it created anyway, returning to hyperspace in a click, where individualised consciousness continued its event-forming. They were able to prove this thanks to advanced instruments made from the very same Nebstron.

As a wonderful consequence of this knowledge, for the first time in human history, wars eventually ceased to flare up as well - enabling the Earth to become its own Type-I civilization).

Tentatively, it was one of the overseers who made a gentle approach to this young and strange mother, (what planet could she possibly be from?) holding out his long hand in silence with a smile. No one knew, in all honesty, *what* she was! That is, to which species she belonged!

The two disjointed-looking children cowered around their curious mother…

What she saw and sensed made *no sense* at all! All her scientific reasoning was attempting to assimilate. Then she watched with high trepidation Peeler Curvature's slightly clumsy approach, monitoring his steady stand-square feet and unusual silver appearance, as coolly as she possibly could.

"It is all right," he said quietly and *very* precisely. "You have nothing to fear. It seems you have somehow been transported to the bridge of our ship, Favola. Welcome. Are they… ah… your children?" He gave a fatherly smile at the two cowering youngsters, who just turned in on their mother for protection. Fatherly perhaps, but no one had children on Favola. All human-species were engendered in test-tubes, then brought up in their relevant infant vicinities with regards to what they were conceived to eventually become. Consequently, the captain did not actually know how to show a parental nature, even though he imagined himself trying. "May I inquire," he went on, "that planet below us-" he gestured with a hand to the massive viewing-platform that was displaying turning oceans outside in graphic blue sunlit close-up, as Favola turned itself silently and slowly across the vast globe, "which is it? Our instruments have no answer." He gently looked back to her, giving a little-boy shrug at one of the kids, while no readings were currently being displayed to Corda, who also smiled.

Shaking, she attempted speech, but was too petrified. Instead, she shook her head, then held her children as one, gazing in almost supernatural wonderment at what she beheld. Though her perception was limited because of her ignorance of the technology, it was wonderment she soon sensed at seeing this craft - at watching the globe. A scientific wonderment, though.

"Sir," Corda then cut in. "Favola informs me that it is Earth, and that the year is…"

"2457!" the woman suddenly gasped, as if shocked herself to hear it.

The captain turned back to the viewing-platform with a descending sense of amazement all over him. "Earth…?" he whispered in a similar wonderment. "But we have… never been… to…"

"Who are you? How… how am I here? Did you say… Favola?" The woman spoke the word as though recalling a poisonous spider or something.

"Quite," said one of the overseers. "And, if you don't mind me asking, what mode of transportation do *you* have?"

"Are you stealing me for some secret project on this new vessel?" she blurted. "I was going to the moon. My brother is throwing a party for the launch! He is part of it all. The moon-mining was only a guise. We were going to watch it shoot off!" She demonstrated this with an arm-wave.

"You know of this project?" said the captain, perplexed at her sudden rambling. "Surely that is impossible. We have already been away from Earth for a thousand years!" He suddenly grasped what year it was - *now*. "Did you say… 2457?" He was marginally daunted.

"Sir," Corda said, "Favola informs me that we are not being detected by Earth's tracking devices, as indeed we should be. Even the number of spacecraft in orbit have not, as yet, seen us. Odd, as we grace them closely. Observe: space-traffic! It is most curious, in my opinion, Captain…"

"Corda, can Favola detect what caused our

time-shift to this space-fabric, as well as how the human transportation in mid-space transpired?" He looked to the woman as if asking forgiveness. He then asked, as she didn't answer the overseer, the name of her mode of transportation again. He edged away from her in kind gestures to give her breathing space.

"We call it, Transdoor," she said, calmer now as she began orientation. Then she said, "My name is Zoe Halloway. I'm a scientist. I had been working *on* the Transdoor myself - along with my many colleagues in atomic heat-flash engineering. I will be missed, however. My brother is expecting me on the moon too, as we speak. As I say. I don't know how I came to materialize on your bridge. I honestly don't. It wasn't intentional. It must have been some kind of anomaly in the Nebstron at home. That's all it could have been!" She fell silent again, still somewhat fearful. "Look," she then asked with forced confidence, "I did not know that they were working on two of these spacecraft - these Favolas! I shall keep it all a secret, if that's what you wish. I had always believed - and it was just a belief mind you - that Favola had been constructed in lunar orbit. Is that true?" She felt conscious of her lies. "Oh please, is there any way you can get me to my destination there? I don't understand why you are in orbit around the Earth. Aren't you due to launch, today?"

"Two, madam?" Corda asked, unsettled.

"We *were* constructed in lunar orbit," the

captain then commented. "But that was a thousand years ago! This, however, was the year of our launch, and we have somehow returned! You see, we have been travelling for a thousand years already, er, Zoc. I am the 20th captain to date! We came across a planet that was curiously imploding from unusual waves of magnetism in the PS-9 galaxy, combined with an unusually intense space-bending heat. 1 quadrillion K, in fact. We were then time-flung into another space-fabric location. It happened quickly. It had never happened before. We were sucked back to the planet, only to be flung again, to here - to Earth. But to the year of our launch? We are as perplexed as you. It is all… most curious." He rubbed his hard chin, then added, "Wormholes? Hmmm. We have the capacity to scan for any possible burgeoning wormholes, if that will help. Monitoring dark-matter as we do allows us to calculate the very forces where we can expect wormholes to form in space!"

"Lines-of-force," the woman half whispered. That's what must have happened to you. "Michael Faraday. His theory. Electrical charges from magnetism can create long lines spreading right across space! That's what he proved, centuries ago. If you connect onto one of them it is possible that you could be instantly moved to any point *in* space. Just like that." She clicked a finger. Then she frowned, and said, "How… can you… monitor dark-matter? It is surely impossible!"

"Impossible? No." The captain became preoccupied.

"We are aware of such things as lines-of-force," Corda then said. "However, we have encountered them before, but not as a direct effect." Looking to the captain. "Perhaps, sir, that *is* what happened to us after all…"

The two overseer-species rose and shuffled towards the scientist and her children attired in gold; this seemed entirely appropriate to Zoe Halloway the scientist, who, by now, was beginning to coldly take-in the Favolan technology surrounding her, even daunting her. The children, though, held onto her slim body, while she caressed their heads individually. "Madam, you say you know of Favola being constructed in lunar orbit? Do you know of anybody who has been aboard the ship? Your, ah, brother perhaps? Maybe there is a way of communicating with him!" The overseer who spoke held his long hands together in front of him in anticipation, watching this curious human being as though watching neutrinos leap about on the cone-screens, as indeed he had done many times before over the centuries. It was fascination he displayed, coupled with a cool, hardly-expressed discomposure…

"Many people don't even believe this ship exists, you know! Let alone two! But you say you have been travelling for a thousand years? How can that be possible? I know about wormholes connecting up different layers of spacetime, but this is crazy!"

"Favola is too big for wormholes," the overseer commented. "Now then, according to our almanac the year is 3457. Our dates simply continued from our launch. We still use Earth-time."

"My god. I can't believe it! This is the future!

"Well, no. *We* are the future. You arc the present. This vessel is… the past."

Again Corda asked of this number 'two.' There was no evidence anywhere that should suggest the construction of two Favolas. None. Corda would have known of such things if there were. *Favola would have known of such things if there were!* And now, as Favola made an attempt at a difficult, unusual mental communication with Corda concerning something which had never come its way before, the big android sat lithely back at its post and fell inert. Zoe the scientist watched its movements with arrant wonder: the robots on Earth did not match the lifelike qualities of this Corda. She was agog. "Sir," it then whispered, "it is imperative that we make the jump into hyperspace now, while we have full control again. Favola informs me that unless we do, we could be sucked into a timeless transaction of galaxy-exchange which would be beyond our control, lasting perhaps… for all time! We must act!"

"Make it so, Corda," the captain reluctantly concurred.

Then Zoe Halloway looked to the two overseers as if for help. "But what about me?" she asked. "I cannot go with you. I have a husband. My children! I cannot go!"

"Madam," one of the overseers said, "we must preserve our world. Corda cannot tell an untruth: if Favola gives the information that we are in danger, then it is so. Prepare yourself for a light-speed leap into another spacetime location. I'm assuming that you have not done it before? It can be a little disorientating. Corda will now determine the amount of curvature present in the hyperspace that we are about to enter. This is vital. Here, let me sit you all in the light-speed enclosure. It should be interesting to you." He beckoned the children as kindly as possible, and an officer came to assist. "It may help if you close your eyes for a few moments as the countdown approaches. We will be billions of kilometres from Earth by the time you open them again, and your body will adjust quickly. It will be all right. We will remain in your galaxy. We will fetch you back to Earth as soon as the light-trajectories are aligned for our size craft. I promise." He then left her to the helping officer.

"Mummy…" one of the children whimpered.

Then, as Favola crested a rim of the great blue planet below, moonrise appeared on the port bow. "Sir," Corda said to the captain as the ship angled towards it, "behold!" He nodded to the viewing-platform, where, in orbit around the moon, Favola's identical double could be seen glinting in the light against the blackness of space. Small at a distance, if not slightly warped in its parallel dimension, it was the ship that was about to be launched - the great dream of generations of scientists and engineers. Their hope of hyperspace travel! And, as it also counted down for its first light-speed hyperspace-leap, the original Favola - the only Favola really - did the same, but in the opposite, moon-dusted direction…

In the exact moment they both vanished into infinity - with different captains at the helm - yet only one Zoe Halloway on board.

CHAPTER FOUR

THE INHABITANTS OF FAVOIA had never bathed in sunlight. As a consequence, along with their nano-blood, they were a healthy shade of grey at all times - except in hyperspace. This alone, to a human who *had* bathed in sunshine, was frightfully disconcerting. And, billions of kilometres from Earth, in the direction of the galaxy's central black hole, Zoe Halloway was frightfully disconcerted…

Favola now cruised at ten-times light-speed on a destination-course for a stable star away from the spiral arm of Earth's galaxy, with Corda at ease while in full control. To a stationary object the craft would only be observed for a nano-second across any horizon, if at all. On board Favola, though, time, imaginary time, at such velocity, had of course virtually stopped, and everything had shrunk to infinitesimal proportions. Literally. At such velocity *General Relativity* made its daunting appearance - combined with the symmetry of advanced superstring theory, (which Earth's scientists up until the mid 22nd century could not fully comprehend) and everything became a tiny, slowed-down version of what it was before light-speed. The inhabitants, though, had no comprehension of this because of the way the universe acted at these levels…

It was a different universe at the speed of light,

as was well known.

Favola could not actually *be* observed, as it was no larger than, say, an average-sized boulder as it streaked through space, yet it actually weighed *more* than it did at full size, as its mass had increased because of the energy generated for the propulsion. And then, on slowing down to a definite halt from the speed of light, Favola expanded to the size of a solar-system for a short period - stretching the fabric of space to accommodate it - before returning to its regular, equally vast, size. This was known as the *Cooling Down Interval* to the inhabitants - even though, as was said, they had no sensation of what was transpiring in their world because it was all relative to the changes in the universe at plus-light-speed. For at those speeds they were also part of the universe's transmutation.

Of course, every hyperspace-leap and its alterations were recorded in Vicinity 20.

In a 4-dimensional reality Favola had not been orbiting the Earth. In a 26-dimensional imaginary-time-related one it had, and this was how the scientist and her two children freakishly came aboard. As she entered Favola's separately-inhabited space-fabric, she and her children had also been transformed in a way. They had become different-dimensional. They would therefore possibly be invisible back on Earth, had they gone directly home. Yes, invisible. Favola itself had worked this out, and had been communicating the data to Corda, as he/she piloted in a big-brained trance. Favola was not there in Earth-time reality, so tracking-devices would not have monitored it. Favola was only there via a multi-dimensional window, and only then via the lines-of-force from the imploding planet, was the message. It had not been there in length, breadth, width, or, as Corda understood it, Earth-time. Though it had been there *in light, and a relative spatial-dimension of motion.* Somehow the Transdoor's Nebstron on Earth had entered this dimension, and gave Zoe up to it.

A youngish, grey scientist-species (merely 200) held out a grey hand with a grey smile to a grey Zoe, who limply took it and smiled back, equally as greyly. She felt positively nauseous after the hyperspace jump and her mass rising/shrinking? as she dreamt it might. Her children had been vomiting on the floor, which the tiny robot-cleaners were already cleaning up in case of alien contamination. A thought had struck her, though, that, as her children sobbed, perhaps these creatures were not human. Or from Earth, anyway. It was a grey situation. Where the hell was she? Had she actually been abducted *by aliens!* Her head was swaying with, as she imagined, the motion from the velocity. There was none, but she felt there was. Stars were white lines coming towards a seemingly stationary Favola, painted along the viewing-platform - quite beautifully, she could perceive in her physical misery. Wow. And look at this Corda thing, handling it so deftly, she thought.

It's… incredible!

Her children, of course, had no concept of the distance they were from their playfriends on Earth: distance? The furthest they'd been was the moon, and that was through the Transdoor which made it seem as though no travelling had taken place! They were currently approaching Alpha Centauri, that, in moments, was behind them as they were en route for yet another solar-system! (While Alpha Centauri was some 4½ light-years from Earth - at just light-speed of course it would take 4½ years to arrive there. Through manipulating hyperspace with Nebstron by pulling it towards Favola in a ten-to-twelve-times light-speed velocity, this made the trip a matter of Earth-minutes. Favola's power-source could distort spacetime by generating enough power and heat to alter the fabric *of* space, by tearing a hole in it large enough to accommodate its girth, thereby giving the effect of space being dragged towards Favola, as though Favola had lassoed it!) Already, some 20 years had zoomed by on Earth. Moments to them, but time *away* from time as it were moved very differently. Think 28-dimensional cubes. In fact a new word had to be made to replace the word *Time* when moving in hyperspace - as well as the concept. Time had no relevance to 'time' in hyperspace! Time only limited things that had existed outside of it. It was of no use. Zoe Halloway had a sense that, at this velocity, they would reach the end of the universe (and time) in a matter of minutes, just about… now. Her knowledge of light-speed, though, and how it might alter 'time' back on Earth for her was, of course, limited - even though she knew a lot about it. For she knew enough to know that electromagnetic fields held atoms and molecules together, and that, at the speed of light, these fields would be instantaneously left behind. Therefore, your atoms and molecules would be left behind, too. Gulp, because, therefore also, the owner of these atoms and molecules would vanish into thick space! The speed of light wasn't the actual velocity of an object - it was instead a maximum speed of the spreading-out of a signal! Glumly, she went to attend to her children…

For what she saw around her was not, it appeared, what the inhabitants of Favola saw. She was, after all, a human being from the planet Earth, circa 2425. Her eyes and brain could only assimilate the shapes and motions related to that planet: her vision of beyond-light-speed outside the spacecraft was 3-dimensional, in that the stars were, as was said, constant white lines moving towards her; but every passing sun never appeared as a sphere. Zoe Halloway's eyes (spheres) were of the Earth. Peeler Curvature's, however, were of Favola, and what he saw at light-speed would no doubt have torn her brain apart. For there were multi-dimensional shapes appearing and then disappearing directly on the bridge. Colours and fabrics which no human had ever known had covered his skin (that grey becoming an alien glint of golden luminosity) before lining the inner-walls to the craft after altering in swirls of visible strings which vanished upwards into a higher level of reality that could never be monitored in the current universe. Everyone saw this, but language couldn't cover it. It was ineffable: normal in hyperspace. It was just… the photon-display of brilliant transmogrification which every conscious creature entering hyperspace over the last ten-million years had witnessed!

Apart from the crew on the bridge, and the sequestered astronomer-species way out all alone on the outer-rim of Vicinity 91 at the rear of the craft, no one knew that Favola had been in a spatial-dimensional orbit around the Earth, or that there were now earthlings on board. Or, that they had been pressed back in time a whole millennium!

The scientist-species then approached Zoe and her children (covered as he was in the colours and fabrics of hyperspace - though without them being able to see it) where she was seated in the light-speed enclosure, and beckoned her to step out. Tentatively, she did. He seemed intelligent enough to perceive her distress; but it was all very amazing, now. *Now* it was amazing. It was all… astonishing! "We have a guest chalet where you and your children can stay," he calmly said. "My name is Ply Prism. I'm afraid you will be with us for a number of your days. You might as well be as comfortable as possible. Let me carry your bag for you. Come. I will lead the way. We have a car waiting."

Leading the way, Ply Prism knew perfectly well that, even by now, she had been away from her husband and friends for a long Earth-time: every minute in hyperspace, he knew, equalled about 10 passing years on Earth. For him it would be all about somehow reversing that time if she had any chance of resuming her old life. But he couldn't allow her to see his anxiety. Also, he knew that Favola had automatically uploaded her brain-patterns without either her knowledge or her consent (was that required?) Each minute-by-minute day of her life had gone into Favola's infinite banks. Consequently, everything *in* that life would presently be available for viewing in Vicinity 20. For some reason, though, Ply Prism wasn't particularly happy about this…

'I'm sorry? What was your name again?" An incredulous Zoe.

"Ply Prism. Are you having problems with your hearing?" He stopped to turn around. He was being genuine with his question. He smiled again at her quite innocently.

"No. I'm fine. Look, er, Mr Prism, are you going to perform experiments on me and my children? We have had reports recently about alien-contact on the moon, and transparent creatures taking people without their consent, then sending them back like damn vegetables!"

"I beg your pardon?"

"Are you going to do things to us? Experiments?" She looked at him.

"Madam, why would we want to experiment on you? We know all about the human being. Earth is where we descended from, after all! That is a strange question for a scientist to ask, I must say. No. I can assure you, you are quite safe. Come, children. You will be able to play like you have never played before!" The children, to Ply Prism, looked absolutely wonderful in their hyperspace glistening, as he led the way to the float-car that would take them to Vicinity 9 - some 12-minutes travelling from the bridge. More pleasant than they did before, he noted. But he couldn't tell them this. They wouldn't have understood anyway, he guessed. They might have panicked, too. No. Best that they saw only whatever it was they *did* see. "Transparent creatures, did you say? I believe they are the conscious energy of dead creatures who now dwell in between the second holographic layer of the universe. Single-dimensional entities, we call them, because they somehow did not fully arrive at the second layer, where everything else that has lived arrives. That is, in that next layer where consciousness becomes tangible matter, and everything realizes that death is in fact an illusion. We have encountered them before. They are mostly harmless. I cannot see how they could abduct anybody as they could not actually touch a 3-dimensional creature! They are but watchers of existence, alas. We have tried to help them whenever we've encountered them. It is a matter of re-aligning their quantum coherence with super strings. This seems to get them where they need to be." Ply Prism's attire glinted like, well, a prism, as he spoke. His face, though, had a sharpness to it that spoke of things beyond Zoe Halloway's understanding, and she knew it. They arrived at the waiting float-car. The children looked amazed at what they saw. They looked for wheels, or, as on Earth now, for hover-jets.

"You mean… ghosts!" she responded with alarm.

"I suppose you could call them that," Ply Prism went on as he placed Zoe's bag in the car, then stood upright and sighed. "Many years ago when I was about 120, we had some of these single-dimensional entities aboard Favola - in Vicinity 50. We studied them for some time, and were alarmed to see that they appeared somewhat stressed, so we attempted help."

Zoe Halloway stared at him hard. "Did you say, 120? My god. How… how… old are you?"

"200, I think. To you I probably look about… 35? Here, just press this button when you're ready, and the car will take you to your destination. It is perfectly safe. You will be met there by a female colleague of mine and shown to your chalet. You might enjoy the trip. Bye bye."

Zoe Halloway watched him wave as the float-car silently moved away from the Bridge-Docking-Bay as though air propelled it, which it probably was - once she'd pressed the button. Her children did not appear as disconcerted as her; to them, now, it was all a game - all play.

The guest chalets were just that: three-bedroom structures along a quiet street in Vicinity 9. In actuality they were guest-quarantine-quarters hermetically-sealed from the rest of the craft. They didn't have roofs, but the cube-like bedrooms, consisting of six curiously altering squares, were only open to the ceiling of Favola many metres above them in an illusory sense. This gave the sensation of circling - if one lay on the bed - which couldn't actually be seen with the naked human eye as it was a type of inert and thick gas. It was, though, extremely comfortable; and once Zoe Halloway had become accustomed to laying herself down on *air* as it were, watching the turning ceiling, she couldn't get enough of it. It was a unique experience. And very relaxing, too. And the children, they bounced on seemingly nothing, half a metre above the floor, a floor that had the appearance of being jagged, but was in fact smoother than polished glass. The chalets could be unravelled if required, where they would fold into a type of 8-dimensional single case-structure that was so light it could be carried by hand then placed on any reasonable planet and lived in for a time. They weren't, needless to say, *chalets* as had been perceived on Earth…

Meanwhile a meeting was being held in the captain's room concerning the fabric of time and Favola's new arrivals *in their new time.* It was a meeting of some concern, as all were privately worried that Zoe Halloway and her children may not be placed back on Earth in the exact time-fabric that they left it. Because she had entered hyperspace, (that is, beyond the first holographic level of reality) there would be, as was said, a major time-shift for her people left behind. As was known, all who entered hyperspace tended not to have relatives on the planet they were leaving, for reasons of time-shifts and the on-going altering fabrics of hyperspace (ie: being somewhere where you literally should not be). Also, her leaving Earth; that, by now, (Favola's now) would have raised alarms. Her brother, as she explained, had been expecting her imminently. They would be attempting to trace her material, as devices had been invented for this purpose in case of emergency, from around the Earth, which, all agreed, was more beautiful than legend had it - more real in its holographic intensity - but in some ways her brother wasn't their problem…

"Even at this point," Ply Prism the scientist explained in the shimmering-sphere of the captain's room, "if we turned around and shot back to the Earth, she would be some 20-to-40 Earth-years ahead of where she originally was! We have to locate a trajectory that would be accurate for her. We must try beyond our best this time…" He lowered his head.

"Quite," said the captain. "Corda has already been instructed to do just that. We will get her back, I am confident. My concern is more how she'll cope with being here, frankly! We must look very strange to her. She does to us, quite obviously. But we to her must seem somewhat, well, threatening? All effort must go into making her feel at case. She is a guest, remember. However, she did not ask to be on Favola, so, in a sense, she has been abducted. This she will no doubt tell when she eventually gets home…" The captain gave a wry smile to the table.

"I agree," the overseer named Xenon Ream concurred. "She appeared highly ncrvous to me. Bizarre as she looks, I felt sorry for her and, indeed, wanted to protect her. However, she will be safe!" He waved a long hand in his usual manner at ending his words. At that moment Favola left hyperspace and all the colour drained from his face. Now grey again, he glanced to a viewing-screen as if recognizing where they were. Favola had slowed right down, and stars had become pinpoints in space once more. The geometric gravity aboard, though, remained the same. "Ah, good," he went on. "Now the clocks have almost equalled. Time has become relevant again for her!"

"Yes," commented Ply Prism. "However, The Cooling Down Interval may have a different effect on her body than it does on ours. We need her molecules to be monitored at all times. Her husband, as we speak, will be some 50 years older than he was when she left him. Indeed he may even have married again and had a family, which could conceivably be old themselves! I am, of course, assuming that the average life-span of a human being on Earth is what - 180, 190? He may even have moved onto the second holographic layer himself by now, and seen everything for what it is - including what truly happened to his wife! Huh. The Metaverse is a strange place…"

"It is indeed," Xenon Ream concurred. "But no matter. It is, I believe, our duty to render this Zoe Halloway and her children back to her original time-fabric and her original life. If we are able to do this, to the precise second, then naturally she will have no memory of us or of Favola. What has transpired to her will not have transpired then. This also is imperative, I feel. Need I remind everyone of our axiom never to harm any life we encounter? No. Of course not. Nor will we. We have a duty!"

"Sir," one of the female officers seriously suggested, "we may have harmed beings unwittingly, simply by disturbing their spacetime with our motion-drives!"

"Hmmm," the overseer gasped, then waved a long hand.

Ply Prism allowed himself a faint grin.

CHAPTER FIVE

A SPECIAL FOOD had to be prepared for Zoe and her two children, Zen, the boy, and Clarest, the girl, as the (illusory) minutes were turning to hours, and food was beginning to be required. They would have to have something to eat during their (long? short?) stay, surely? So, Favola deemed that they should be served a kind of special protein dish (the texture of putty) with freshly grown, unusually shaped vegetables in their chalet, by two members of the chef-species, who had been directed how to cook it all, with their noses as wide as wildebeest on Earth…

The inhabitants of Favola got their sustenance from a myriad varieties of soup-paste, made from fish to grass to all sorts of things - *by* the chef-species. They couldn't eat solids, as their nano-run bodies couldn't really break them down, and, as they didn't require them, solids were never on the menu.

Thus, after a period of unsuspected quarantine in the chalets of Vicinity 9, where the two children had discovered the float-belts which they used to amuse themselves by hovering around the area Peter Panlike, Zoe Halloway ate the local food on board a massive spaceship that was circling close to her galaxy's awesome centre - a view she would never see. She was told later that she could visit one or two other vicinities, where the human-species involved had been warned what to expect, but that was all. A nervously-friendly alien guest and her unusual offsprings, ambling around? No. Zoe tentatively spooned strange textures into her mouth, as her body crested over a vision of outer-space magnificence below which would forever elude her.

Favola moved magically, already examining every single molecule in the three bodies, and checking them against the molecules of the thousands of inhabitants. They were fine - except for Zen. The astronomer-species would, had they ventured outside of Vicinity 91 and made contact with Zoe, (something they would never regret doing) received an unpleasant gut-bug from him. The astronomer-species were known across generations for their sequestered condition. They didn't mix, and so they didn't catch anything. But when they did, (which was rare) they went down heavily - even though there was nothing *to* catch on Favola. So they remained remote but, as they perceived it, heathly - one eye much larger than the other - scanning as they did each and every civilization they came across, in each and every scanned galaxy, consisting, they knew, of around 200 *billion* stars. Favola moved magically.

The astronomer-species had worked out that, on average, intelligent life was about 15 light-years apart from each other in every galaxy. Unfortunately, it tended to evolve at thousands of years either before or after other intelligent life-forms, so that they either wiped themselves out before they became Type I civilizations, or that, by eventually becoming Type II civilizations, they wiped other lesser civilizations out as a bored earthling might flush ants from a garden path with water in the dark past. This seemed to be happening a lot in the universe, the astronomer-species had noted…

Type III civilizations abounded in the cosmos, they knew.

They had informed Corda to divulge to Zoe Halloway that a Type III civilization was already established in her own galaxy - but kindly-Corda was reluctant to tell her this. The Type III would no doubt wipe her civilization out before it grew any more powerful in its Type I status, they deduced. And, had they met her, they would have given Zoe their solemn condolences…

Type III civilizations were established in most galaxies that Favola had encountered. They could harness inter-galactic travel by capturing, as had been said, the power of every sun *in* their galaxy, using this power as one gigantic whole. Conseqently, they could run machines that would be beyond a Type II cilivilzation's comprehension, or, if needs be, defeat. Hence Earth's probable demise. The overseer-species had observed that governments of Type O civilizations constantly prevented their inhabitants from *becoming* Type I, by, strangely enough, inventing differences that appeared to matter to the various populations.

These differences were then perceived as such *by* the inhabitants, thus the inhabitants were maintained in an invented detestation of their fellow creatures, all thanks to their owned rulers, who themselves acted under orders. The overseer-species found this curious, and had even written laughable poems about it which they occasionally recited at public hearings in the forests. For it appeared to be a prerequisite of a Type 0, before it ever became a Type I. This, to the overseers, had a certain irony about it.

The astronomer-species, on the other hand, had guessed, from the information they'd been given, that Zoe Halloway was a creature of a Type O civilization, which had just become a Type I. They suspected, though, that she was probably a Type I creature herself all along, as indeed many people were in Type O civilizations. For they had monitored many in their slightly spooky vicinity, way out on the rim there, all alone.

The scientists and engineers who designed and constructed Favola a thousand years ago, while living, as Zoe herself, in a Type O civilization on the verge of Type I, were themselves people of a Type II civilization really, and, Favola itself, while being a spaceship of a Type II civilization created by them, was probably a craft more suited to an incipient Type III, of which the astonomer-species aboard knew of a most amazingly advanced one - in, of course, the Andromeda galaxy. Every star there had already been harnessed and had been used for some two-thousand of Earth's years. This meant that Favola was, in fact, a craft on the leading edge of design in the known universe, (even by 3457 standards – known being relative, of course) and that Corda, in full control of it at all times (Corda never slept) was a sentient being of the calmest superiority. *Or,* so it would subjectively seem to Zoe's eventual speculation. Favola was, really, in some senses a massive thinking computer. It was somehow evolving towards receiving its energy from the many stars that it/she moved over, *or* even transgressed. In fact the old on-board 28th-generation computers had made themselves almost obsolete; together they had transformed Favola into what she was becoming: a living, thinking, vast being, unique in the universe. Different, then, to that of a Type III civilization, as it operated alone.

Gzzzzzzz! Zoe felt a mild electrical shock hit her feet as she stepped out of Vicinity 9, accompanied by Ply Prism the scientist. He was leading her, now that she'd had sustenance, to her first visit: one of the pleasure-domes, via a float-car. There was something he wanted to show her. No, there was a lot he wanted to show her. And the children too. Zoe seemed to be bringing a fresh wonderment to him regarding his own environment. "I've just had an electric shock," she told him.

Turning, he looked to the children. No. They hadn't had one, it was clear. What was Favola doing, he vaguely thought? "It could just be electromagnetism," he suggested. "There's no problem. Anyway, we have what you might call miniature light-cones in the particular pleasure-dome I'm taking you to," Ply Prism suggested. "They're great fun. You allow yourself to drop into it from a type of slide, then the light beams actually pick you up and fire you in an imaginary light-second to the other side of the dome, where you can look at yourself being fired because you've arrived before you've even left! Then, while on the other side in a second version *of* yourself, you get a clearer vision of how your brain works, as, in effect, you are somebody else! Come. Let me show you." He then pressed the float-car's button and off it floated - to the pleasure-dome.

"Light-cones?" Zoe questioned. "How can a beam of light pick up solid flesh?"

"Well, it's not really light. But we call them light-cones. It's actually a 12-dimensional electron gun, which literally shoots your molecules into a multi-dimensional reality via a drug-induced hyperbolic state." He smiled at her as the car moved along the highway.

"A what?"

"A hyperbolic state. That is, an outer-body-hovering for a short time. We need it occasionally."

"Why would you need an outer-body experience on a spacecraft? It doesn't make sense. Look, I'm not taking any drugs. I'm not even supposed to be here. I feel a bit funny now." She sat in the rear of the vehicle, holding her children, who, again, did not appear to be disconcerted in the least by it all.

Then Zen, Zoe's son, said, "This car isn't making any noise!" as though being the only one who recognized the fact. "Hey mister, what's making it go?"

The float-cars had no steering wheel or panel, just a location-director and a go-button. But Ply Prism, who was sitting where a steering wheel might have been, turned to the boy and declared that it was, "Magnetism and kinetic energy! You see, Favola is a great big sphere of kinetic power!"

"Oh," said Zen. "Well, can it go any faster?"

"Yeah!" said his sister, "Let's go faster!"

"They cannot go any faster than this," said the ever-calm Ply. "They are programmed vehicles without any engines. This is the only motion they have."

"Mummy," said Clarest after a pause, gazing up at the blue sky, "where are we?"

"I don't really know, darling," said Zoe. "I think we're close to the moon."

The logical Ply Prism corrected her. "No. We're close to the black hole at the centre of your galaxy, I believe!" He glanced back as if to acknowledge the correction with a smile. Clarest the girl began to whimper at that news. She didn't know what it meant, but it sounded bad.

"No, the moon," Zoe corrected him. "We're

close to the moon, darling." At that moment, as if to appease the little girl, the neon-lit pleasure-dome came into view from along the dusky highway. It struck Zoe Halloway as something she might have seen on Earth - a virtual fun-palace of some description, only different. There appeared to be a lot of activity around the silver entrance. People, or, as far as Zoe could tell they were *people,* were coming and going, but silently. They appeared happy enough, but they weren't making any noise, unlike back home. As the float-car pulled up outside and stopped, Zoe's two children began laughing and giggling at these different types of people walking around. There were members of the maintenance-species, with their 18 long fingers and straight faces. There were members of the entertainer-species, with their fixed grins and delirious eyes. There were also one or two members of the doctor-species - those odd characters with actual lights fitted to their skulls. Yes, it was all highly amusing, to the two children…

"What we have here on Favola are pulsar-credits," Ply Prism then informed Zoe Halloway, as they climbed from the stationary car with ease. "Each of us gets so many pulsar-credits a month, and we use them as we please. For example, it costs 10 credits to enter this particular pleasure-dome, where everything inside is available at that exchange…"

"Money, you mean!" Zoe cut in.

"No. Not money like you used to have on Earth. The pulsar-credits cannot be saved in a bank or anything, nor can they be invested. They are strictly for use only for concepts like this."

Zoe held her children as they stood before the enormous (it looked like silver but was in fact metallic-blue) pleasure-dome, where distant hums and thunder-crashes could be heard from within. She didn't feel good about it. In fact, she actually felt afraid as she had done as a child. "Why isn't everything just for free?" she then asked Ply Prism.

"... I don't know," he eventually gasped. "We've, ah, never questioned it. Some things *are* for free. You can walk in the forests for free, for instance. Or swim in the rivers. You can ride the float-cars for free. But that's all. Everything else costs you pulsar-credits. But it's all right. We will never run out of them and we don't really earn them. Here, take one. Have a look at it." He handed her a glass-like coin, which pulsed with purple light. "That is a 10-credit pulsar-piece! You can tell by the colour. Just place it in that slot, and I may go inside. Favola has already programmed it that you and your children will be freepeople in your stay here. You can go inside for nothing!" He looked startled, oddly.

Zoe relaxed a little, but was still uneasy about all the people staring at her and her children. They did, after all, look like curious monsters to the inhabitants - who could view each side of their faces simultaneously. Think split-mirrors. Then a doctor-species made an approach to Ply Prism, and whispered something in his ear. Zoe was about to place the light-coin in the slot for him, but stopped herself when she saw this doctor. Although she didn't know he was a doctor, he looked, to her, as if he might have knowledge in that sort of area, re personal images of such…

Ply Prism looked carefully at Zen, the boy, then back at Zoe. "The doctor," he said, "would like a word with you, if that's all right. Doctor. Please."

"Hello," said this doctor very tentatively, "my name is doctor Firmation. I have something to tell you, if I may. Corda has just informed me, via Favola, that your son here has the beginnings of what you might call a brain-tumour. If I may, I would like to remove it for him before he goes inside the pleasure-dome. He may experience some vertigo if I don't. Would that be okay?" Doctor Firmation gazed at Zoe Halloway's multi-sided face with intense fascination, awaiting an answer.

She fell cold. "I beg your pardon? My son has what!"

"He has the beginnings of a brain-tumour. But it is nothing to be concerned about, I assure you. Here, allow me to run my hymnus over the side of his head where the tumour is located, and that will be an end of it. The hymnus will eradicate any infected tissue. I promise, it is entirely painless."

"You can do that? You can remove a brain-tumour while we stand here, in front of all these, ah, people! No! I won't let you! My God. How do I know you're telling me the truth? I want another consultation. Ply, tell this man to go away!"

Ten or so human-species were now watching, quietly. "If Favola has told Doctor Firmation that Zen has a tumour, then it is so, Zoe. He is not lying, nor would he. Only children on Favola get brain-tumours through a contamination which we cannot trace. But we can easily remove them. Look, if I ask the doctor to show you his instrument, will that be all right? It is a fascinating machine. Yes. Thank you, doctor. See, Zoe, the hymnus!" Ply Prism held a thin black cylindrical object up to Zoe, not much longer than his hand. He touched the side of his own head with it, then called Zen over from his mother's embrace.

"Zen." said the doctor, "That is a nice name. What do you think of this, Zen? Here, feel it vibrate! It tickles if you comb your hair with it. Have a try."

Zen took the hymnus without hesitation and rubbed it over his head without a word. He looked to Zoe for guidance, but she now seemed okay with the idea. "Ha-ha. Yeah! It feels funny! It tickles! Mom, can I have one? Oh, please. Can I?" The doctor gently took the hymnus from Zen, and glanced at its glowing tip. "That's fine," he then commented with a smile. "Your boy no longer has a tumour! I'm sorry to have troubled you."

"Well, thank you, doctor," Zoe then whispered to the doctor's back.

"No harm done," said Ply Prism. "Now then. Let's take a look inside the pleasure-dome!"

CHAPER SIX

FAVOLA HAD RECORDED THAT, back at the newly-forming imploding planet, which was many light-years from their present location, the intense heat had actually been fluctuating just before the last time-fling. At one point Favola had monitored it approaching 10 K - hot enough to distort spacetime. There seemed no doubt now that this was the reason for the time-fling.

But why had Favola not returned to Earth in a thousand years?

Meanwhile, on approaching the black hole at the centre of the Milky Way Galaxy, Corda was slowly aligning the great craft for a light-speed shoot through. Indeed, Favola had deemed that it was vital to enter the black hole in order to escape the lines-of-force which were still connected - even from another galaxy. Once through, they would be on the other side of the universe: no longer in the deadly grip. What Favola, though, that great big thinking computer, was not taking into account, and how could it, was the fact that the Type III civilization which was already established *in* Earth's Milky Way Galaxy, (the galaxy which Favola referred to as JXI6) and which had had a probe *on* Earth since about the year 1066, (underwater, in the Red Sea) was monitoring *it*. For only now had Favola detected the Type III's 10-dimensional beings who were aboard - even though it couldn't discern what sort of beings they were. *Alien Intrusion,* it had told Corda, (and placed the alert) who could not detect them anywhere in the 91 vicinities. They were, even within Favola, *undetectable,* as such.

Of the 300 billion or so stars in each and every galaxy in the universe, only around 200,000 of them had orbiting planets which were the right size and distance from their suns for life to evolve, the astronomer-species had documented. And of those 200,000 only about half that number came with 'intelligent' life. By the time a Type III civilization got to establish itself in a galaxy, probes from Type I's in the same galaxy would have also begun expanding horizons. Example: Earth's civilization had been sending probes successfully beyond its own solar-system from about the year 2410, and the probes had been reporting back. The probes from the Type III civilization in Earth's galaxy, meanwhile, while harnessing every sun (including Earth's, naturally), were reporting back this information to them. And, as the Type I began finally harnessing its sun's energy directly, the Type III would have detected a small drop from that particular power-source: it would have investigated. Disguised as large rocks, their myriad probes could pinpoint the exact planet of siphoning, and report back that it was a Type I civilization. The Type III civilization, in whichever galaxy, would not allow the lesser one to advance any further - for reasons of exclusive pleasure mostly - and the planet would then be silenced forever. Blip. Just like that. Gone. No more siphoning from that planet's sun!

The 'rock' probe on Earth had never been observed, because it was just that to look at: a rock. But it had been monitoring every movement on the planet since early times. There was also a probe on the moon, and other probes too on every planet and moon throughout the Milky Way. For a millennium there had been probes on moons and planets throughout the entire galaxy from the Type III civilization which was established there!

Xenon Ream the overseer, who knew the above information, had been expressing concern once more about Zoe and her children. Indeed, it did appear at one stage that he was getting in a flap about it. "Remember that earthling?" he ranted to Peeler Curvature on the bridge. "What was his name now? Erm… Leonardo Da Vinci! Yes! That was it! Remember how we were told that a Type II craft came to Earth from a planet in the Virgo supercluster, and took him from his own time? What was the year now? Erm… 2010! Yes! That was it! He was a young man in 2010. Remember how they returned him 550 years into Earth's dark past, all alone? Terrible thing. Who knows how the poor man coped with that! Well, we are not, I repeat, *not,* going to do that to our guest! With my last breath I will get her back to the exact moment - the *exact* moment, mind - so that she can resume her life. That is my promise to her!" He waved a long hand.

"Quite, my old friend," said the captain. "Corda is presently working on that promise through Favola. The Leonardo story is an interesting story, however, Xenon. I too was told this as a child. We all were. Leonardo, the story goes, spent the rest of his life *drawing* the things which gave him comfort - the things he would never see again! Fascinating. Remember how we were told that the humans later regarded him as a man ahead of his time! How true! He was! Literally!" Peeler Curvature gave a chuckle to Corda at that mirth; but Corda, inert at the helm, did not respond.

"Yes!" gasped the overseer. "That is correct! That's how the story ends! Miraculous!" Xenon Ream then went calmly on observing Peeler Curvature at his post, suddenly seriously.

Who moved closer to Corda. "How far are we from the galaxy's black hole, Corda?" he then methodically asked, edging over to the viewing-platform on his square feet to stand by it.

"The galaxy's black hole is almost upon us, captain. It should be in view. In fact, there it is! Observe!" Corda directed the captain's gaze to a white line of light being taken from a near-by star into the invisible black hole, just off the starboard bow. Compared to the star, the black hole doing the pulling was unusually small. Its distance was less than a thousand kilometres from Favola's stationary location. The black hole, however, had no pull on the craft: only the four shudders would be felt.

"How much longer before we can align for entry?" the captain then asked.

"Imminent, sir. All that is required now is our initial angle."

"Fine, Corda. Take us closer at: sharp, 23. Angle. 61. That should be close enough to receive and overthrow the shudder. Motion-drives - off-forward. 106. Angle. 70. Steady. Keep to 70. That is the angle of entry." At that moment the 'shudder' which Peeler Curvature mentioned, transpired. Four small tremors followed each other throughout the entire ship - perfectly symmetrical, perfectly normal on closing on a powerful black hole. But that was all. Only four. Hardly noticeable really. Zoe Halloway felt them, and so did everybody else: all hands had been informed that Favola was about to enter a black hole via their ear-implants. It was standard procedure. But the tremors were no more than minor trembles. "Good," said the captain. "That takes us beyond - to the alignment. Once through the shudders we're almost on the other side!"

"Sir," said Corda after a moment, "Favola is now perfectly positioned for a hyperspace-leap through the black hole. I have set the coordinates for our exit. We will emerge in the star-system WT15, on the edge of the JX78 galaxy."

"Perfect!" Xenon Ream declared in the background.

"Excellent, Corda," said the captain. "Bring it

into being."

Favola had known for a millennium that at the dead centre of a black hole was an instant in time, and not a space-location. It knew that the centre of a black hole was a frozen moment of how the universe was when the partcular star which formed it collapsed. So, on firing through this frozen moment at infinite velocity, part of the moment would somehow remain with Favola until Favola entered *another* black hole that was older than the previous one. It would then shed the initial moment-in-time while gaining an *older* moment that somehow negated the earlier one, while also simultaneously endowing Favola's entirety with a unique and special knowledge of how the universe acted and mutated from its inception. Consequently, Favola was dropping off moments-in-time everywhere, to regain *different* moments-in-time at many points all around the universe. This was becoming a type of personal quest. Cause and effect? Favola was growing, via every black hole it entered. Favola was learning.

Corda paused (for a moment), and frowned. Turning to a lighter shade of green, he/she then looked to the captain as if in apology. "Sir, Favola now informs me that, as we still have Alien Intrusion Alert, it would be dangerous for us to carry them with us. Favola says that they are beings from the type III cvilization which controls Earth's Milky Way Galaxy. They would no doubt be… well, missed. We must somehow track them down. Favola fears a possible retribution for their abduction to a galaxy where they might not be welcome."

"Retribution, Corda?" the captain asked.

"Yes, sir. Beings from Type III civilizations tend to be, as we know, at hyper-war with beings from *other* Type III civilizations - for overall dominance of the universe! We have no evidence of their battles of course, but there *is* evidence of stars being shut down before the natural end of their lives. The astronomer-species have long since suspected foul play with these stars…"

"Yes, but that's the astronomer-species, Corda," the captain said. "The beings who are aboard Favola now came aboard by their own effectuation. They were not invited aboard. It is vital that we leap through this black hole in front of us-" he looked at it, "otherwise, we could be in an even greater danger! The transgressors can look after themselves. No one will be seeking retribution. What is getting into Favola?" He looked behind to Xenon Ream as if for an answer.

"Sir," Corda went on, "Favola also informs me that we are presently being scanned by the Type III civilization here in the Milky Way! Observe!" Corda pulled its hands away to show the captain a tiny diamond probe drifting across the instrument panel.

"Scanned?" Xenon Ream questioned, looking.

"Yes, sir. Favola says that we have been monitored ever since we were in orbit around the

Earth - by the same civilization! Indeed, they have members aboard as we speak, and Favola says that this is a scanning device!" Corda waved a hand over it as it moved.

"I wish to meet with these people!" Xenon Ream then forcefully demanded. "Let us go to their planet now and meet with them! We will not be *scanned!*" He went to wave a long hand, but Peeler Curvature stepped in front of him and seemed to prevent it.

"We do not know where their planet is, sir," Corda then gently commented.

"Quite," said Peeler Curvature, watching the diamond probe for the first time. "Why have we not seen this before? How long has it been aboard?" He watched it intently. Then, a thought seemed to come over him. "I am beginning to find it strange that we have not been back to Earth since our initial launch," he felt the need to say. "Why has it never been a priority for Favola to return? I don't understand. It should have been. In fact we should have been making regular visits to Earth! Tell me why, Xenon? We knew the coordinate. Why didn't we return?" He gazed directly at the overseer as though searching for a conspiratorial twitch or something.

"... Well," Xenon Ream gasped while looking beyond Peeler Curvature to the awesome vision of the black hole sucking light and energy from the near-by star, then back at the tiny diamond probe floating throughout the gleaming bridge, "it seems that we were not programmed to. That is, Favola's mission was to keep going, and to record everything along the way. Which indeed we do, as we know - in Vicinity 20 - but only for the inhabitants *of* Favola. Now then, to return to Earth would have been in some respects a breach of our eternal mission." He silenced himself to watch the probe again, which appeared to be hypnotic. "Fascinating," he whispered at it.

"Nonsense!" declared the captain. "We could have easily reported our findings to Earth's scientists on a regular basis. That is, I am sure, what they would have wished for. No. There must be something more. There must be another reason why we have never returned to Earth before recent events. It has been wrong of us."

"Wrong?" said Xenon Ream. "Captain, you are stepping over your boundary!"

"No, Xenon. It is my duty to question what Favola does on occasion."

"Well, that's as may be, but I am giving you a warning."

"Warning? I am the captain of Favola! I am doing my duty! Look, why were we flung back to Earth? There must have been a reason. What power in the universe could have directed us back to our place in time, as it were. It was awesome what transpired, Xenon. Awesome. You saw it. We could have gone anywhere in the cosmos, but we didn't. We were directed back to Earth. There is something going on. I feel it. And I am going to find out what…" He shuffled across to Corda, who appeared slightly unsettled by the two men's altercation.

Xenon Ream, who did not like either being shouted at or silenced in mid sentence, went to sit down in the light-speed enclosure. He appeared highly troubled.

"Sir," Corda then broke in, "Favola informs me that it is highly probable that the beings who are currently with us from the Type III civilization, engineered it for us to be shot back to Earth. It was not, it seems, the imploding planet's lines-of-force. This is the latest data. Favola is also suggesting that…" he paused to take this in, "they sent us home because… we haven't been there before? This seems highly irregular, I know. Favola is suggesting that the Type III beings are… well, playful. They are, it seems, playful beings, sir. This probe is, apparently, a thought-inducer, and not, as we first believed, a probe…" Corda looked at it, curiously.

"'"A thought-inducer?" said Xenon Ream, sulking slightly.

"What!" said the captain. "Corda, begin the countdown for the shoot through! These *playful* beings of yours can come along for the ride - if it so amuses them! Bring it into being." The captain sat in his central chair in the centre of the room and held onto the bone-like arm-rests.

Favola then powerfully fired its motion-drives for a single shoot through the black hole - no questions asked. However, was the probe inducing this notion in him, or was he acting independently? He did not have the wherewithal to think these thoughts, nor did he look behind at Xenon Ream, who, it appeared, was definitely visually sulking, bottom lip thrusting outward.

CHAPTER SEVEN

ZOE HALLOWAY ENTERED THE PLEASURE-DOME, as Favola entered the black hole.

This time there was a sensation: the black hole's electromagnetic ultra-pull somehow seemed to twist her ankles. As she and her children stepped forwards through the wide entrance, to be greeted by primed members of the entertainer-species (think circus on Earth, circa 1970) who, while floating slowly on animated trajectories, welcomed the children as well to a wonderland of hi-tech magic, her ankles seemed to bend around each other in a painless twist of contortion. She let out a yell, and looked down. But they appeared okay.

No pain, just the sensation of being twisted.

Odd, as she'd twisted them before for real while riding a hover-bike on Earth. Then, the sensation was the same, but the pain was excruciating. No pain here, just a twisting-feeling of bones bending backwards like rubber, of bones bending behind each other like steel, bones bending into shapes which they'd never bent to before. Yet she could walk perfectly okay.

"It's all right," Ply Prism advised her as they entered the dome properly, with his arm around her shoulder. "Favola has already travelled the 30,000 light years from Earth, and has just entered the black hole at the centre of your galaxy. It's an amazing craft, you know. And… now, it has just left the other side! We are probably about five-million-light-years from Earth's space-location! I believe you are the only human in the history of humanity to be so far away. How does it feel?" He gave a big smile. This smile seemed all the more weird in its pleasure-seeking setting.

Zoe was doubly daunted. Times twenty. The pleasure-dome's interior structure seemed to be constructed entirely of liquid, in that it moved with every move you made - seemingly to suit your move. It was transparent; yet from the outside it appeared to be constructed of metal, and freestanding. Indeed the area of its location was a lot larger than the dome itself, and Zoe could see whole sections of Favola's interior beyond it. It reminded her of an open scene in the Arizona Desert, only under a different light. It seemed sandy, and hilly, with plantlife and (synthetic) sunshine. Most strange. The ambience, to her, was vaguely of dusk in a wide horizon. There was music playing, using not just the 12-tone row but a 28-tone row; people were doing the strangest things to it. They were… well, floating! Floating while… seemingly dancing. An odd dance, though. Second daunting: "I've… we've… me… we've just gone through a black hole? You are kidding. It can't be. I *don't* - didn't - believe it was possible! On Earth people still believe that it cannot be done! Nothing could survive it, surely?" She looked to Ply Prism with a questioning frown.

"It's true!" he said. "We only hit light-speed momentarily, however. Indeed we are probably motionless now, or travelling very slowly. Did you get a sensation of your ankles twisting? We all get that. That's how you know. That's the feeling. That's the feeling you get when you go through a black hole! It's the only pull we get whenever we go through one. But the moment-in-time, which will now be with us, that's a different matter altogether. It should take hold shortly. The moment-in-time is a rather odd phenomenon: it causes us all to dream the exact same dream, at the precise moment. This dream then gets logged and discussed interactively in the forests at a later date."

"The moment in time?"

"Yes. As you no doubt know, the centre of a black hole is not the singularity as was believed up until the 21st century on Earth, but the captured moment of when the star that formed it fell in on itself. As Favola flashes across this moment, it takes part of its higher-dimensionality. The ancient fragment of the cosmos slips into everybody's unconscious, then, displayed there as one vision! Sounds strange, I know. You will probably experience it too when you sleep. It's actually very pleasant." Ply Prism watched happily some of the human-species dance in mid air to this very peculiar music. "Also," he then added, "Favola can sometimes suspend itself just above the event horizon, motionless. What we've discovered is that the event horizon of a black hole is a precise time-machine. You can get off at any spacetime location since the black hole's formation! One minute's suspension? 10 Earth-years."

Zoe watched him, perplexed. "So… you could get me home?" She felt the need to ask. She pinched herself. "Is this… all a dream?" She glanced down at her dreamlike children, who watched her, dreamily. They seemed real enough.

"Not as far as I can tell," said Ply. "Favola is as real as it gets in the holofield!"

"Oh. I see. Okay. Very well. Tell me, then, who, or what, are those four tall creatures standing over there, next to that spinning diamond thing, looking like, well, something from a nightmare?" Zoe pointed to the four (was it four?) 10-dimensional beings who were surreptitiously aboard Favola, and were now in the pleasure-dome, observing all the pleasure.

Ply Prism looked to where she pointed. "Which creatures?"

"Those creatures, there, writhing in white! Are they human-species from the engine-room or something? They look very weird to me. They're very tall for an engine-room, if they are."

"We don't have engine-rooms on Favola. And I don't see four creatures anywhere! Where are you pointing'?" He followed her finger.

"Ply, just there! Right next to that spinning glass thing!"

"You mean, the Chromatic Bone-Splinterer?

You must try that. It's very exhilarating. It does things to your bones that you may not have felt before! Okay. There is no one next to the Chromatic Bone-Splinterer. You must be suffering a visual side-effect from the shoot through the black hole. That's what it is. I can get you attended to right away. Come. We can see an eye-specialist now." He was serious.

"I'm fine!" Zoe looked to her children. "Look, Zen, can you see those four shapes? Clarest, can you, darling? See? Where mummy's pointing? Yes. The white people?"

Both children nodded, but were much more taken with the various rides of the pleasure-dome than some silly old white things writhing in a corner.

"But… I don't see anything!" Ply Prism declared. Then Corda spoke to him in his ear-implant. "Sir, I am now able to locate the aliens from Earth's JXlO galaxy. It appears that they are in the pleasure-dome, where you are. Do you have a visual on them? My detector shows that you are the nearcst to them of all the inhabitants." Ply Prism held his ear as if to confirm what he'd just heard through it, then looked again. Nothing. He could not see the 10-dimensional beings from the Type III civilization in Earth's galaxy. "Corda, I do not have a visual on them. But, ah, Zoe Halloway and her two children do. They can see them! According to her, there are four of them, and they are standing, or, as she says, *writhing,* directly next to the Chromatic Bone-Splinterer, perhaps taking something from it. Does the captain wish me to take any action? Zoe must be able to see them because of the dimensional differences from Earth's surface to here." After a pause, Corda said that that was a negative. "Take no action, the captain said."

"Look, mummy," said Zoe's little girl Clarest. "The white things are floating through that doorway. Ha-ha-ha. Isn't that funny!" She pointed in a happy manner.

"Which doorway?" Ply Prism asked, concerned.

The girl pointed to a hermetically-sealed door that led to a virtual-ride at nano-proportions through the body of a living creature. The ride began in the creature's mouth, and ran through the veins to the brain. It was a very popular ride with the doctor-species, especially. For the creature was humanoid. One sat in a car-type container that rocked, and the ride commenced. Zoe lost sight of the 10-dimensioanl creatures after that. Then Corda told Ply Prism not to pursue them - not that he could.

There was one particular chamber which Ply Prism wished to show Zoe Halloway in the pleasure-dome: the *Video-Cam-On-Ancient-Games,* chamber. He felt she'd enjoy it.

One of Favola's major discoveries over its thousand-year journey was that a natural time-bubble could be created from dark-matter at a certain point in its space-formation mode, outside of galaxies. It could only happen at the exact precision-point. A human-species could be safely carried to any location of spacetime in history, or the future - while remaining in their own period. It was a bit like a Transversible Wormhole, in that the bubble (or wormhole) is formed from intense heat and is somewhat delicate; but the time-travel is more precise because the time-bubble is 10-dimensional and actually controlled. Locked in the chamber in the Video-Cam-On-Ancient-Games, the time-traveller then experiences the trip second-hand, as it were - though it is infinitely real thanks to the advancement of the recording devices used in the time-bubble. It wasn't just a cinematic invention. It was a 6-dimensional recording from the 10-dimensional time-bubble of a chariot-race in ancient Rome on Earth, say, or a behemoth-ride in the oceans of the planet Cremona in a solar-system in the Andromeda galaxy way into the future, as that planet evolved. You felt that you were there.

Many things had been recorded thanks to the time-bubbles. This was the only contact human-species had had with their home planet. It had caused a number of them to ask for a return.

On Earth in ancient times for instance the Red Sea *was* parted, but from the gravitational pull of a close-passing asteroid; and this had been recorded. Most human-species on Favola had watched the phenomenon thanks to the Video-Cam-On-Ancient-Games. The time-bubble was beyond the constraints of the laws of physics. Indeed Favola had discovered that its very existence *queried* the laws of physics - even the laws which were scientifically advanced by the year 3457. For the time-bubbles could be maintained by Favola, all over the cosmos, once they were brought into being. They just needed to be located. No mean task, however. For it was a question of knowing *where* to locate them - in the area where they dwelled in the size of space between galaxies? Something the size of a double-bed in this space? (That was where dark-matter did most of its work, the astronomer-species had noted - the space in between galaxies). Unfortunately for Zoe Halloway - although she wasn't thinking along these lines - the time-bubble could not take you back to a certain period and drop you off. You remained in your own time, and were simply a sightseer to the other time and planet, totally invisible to all you saw. You couldn't touch, as it were. You could only look. You were a sealed guest of your own time, in *another time.* Hence how you couldn't get hurt, because nothing could touch *you.* The time-bubble was safe in that respect. Vehicles would drive straight through you. Monsters would bite beyond you. Winds and storms would blow around you, both in the video-show and the bubble itself, where it required an experienced pilot.

For the time-bubbles were controlled. And this was where the inhabitants of Favola got the idea of

Video-Cam-On-Ancient-Games! As only a few human-species could actually use the time-bubbles, (navigator-species, officer-species, the occasional overseer-species who had taken the trouble to learn how) it was eventually decided that a record could/should be made of every trip - backwards or forwards - where a chair was then designed to give the virtual sensation of shifting through the fabrics of spacetime from which things had been witnessed first hand.

CHAPTER EIGHT

ZOE HALLOWAY HAD NO DESIRE to try out the Video-Cam-On-Ancient-Games chamber. She felt she didn't have the capacity for it. Or, she felt she might be removed from time in it, as it were, as indeed she already had been. No, she further felt that she was in a definite, tangible world which her dreams had definitely tangibly created for her, and which, like Earth's electromagnetic field back home - the ground-base of her local hologram - now held within cold, infinite darkness. Therefore, she told herself, she could no longer feel anything. Zoe Halloway had no real idea of where she was…

Plus, the ethereal putty dish she ate, whilst sweet and tasty enough, was beginning to repeat on her. She had been burping its odd, somewhat glue-like flavours into her nose. Burp! Pardon.

Ply Prism, on the other hand, in not burping at all, had the overwhelming desire placed in his head (possibly by the diamond-probe thought-inducer) to look inside the Nano-Prop-Virtual-Ride, of which he did, to see if he could locate the white 10-dimensional creatures. Something was driving him, he felt. Something other than his own mind. It was for scientific reasons, he then reassured himself with. The ride was something he didn't particularly like, however. It had a highly disorientating effect, even when the spectator was prepared for what would take place - which indeed Ply Prism was not. It could also induce mild nausea. And what if the creatures were there? What then? What, indeed, *was* a 10-dimensional creature in this holographic universe?

Gravity's electrical magnetism caused the warping of spacetime, he knew, as it bent and distorted the fabric of space when moving invisibly through it via a solid body. Therefore, his reasoning went, gravity *and* magnetism, as well as all the electromagnetic fields, were multi-dimensional, so beings who existed in these higher dimensions would perhaps be the same. His scientist's mind had already gripped him and told him to boldly go. It was probably playing tricks, but, before Zoe could say: Take me home, Ply Prism had boldly gone. He walked towards the door where the children had said the white creatures had drifted through, then opened it. It made a suction noise, as normal. He stepped through. Ply Prism then vanished from Favola. Or so it seemed. He wasn't sure if he'd fallen directly into the Nano-Prop-Virtual-Ride, as he'd shrunk to nano-proportions before he could even think! That's how it appeared, anyway. He had, to all intent and purposes, vanished!

There were particles older than the universe itself in there - ergo, another universe had existed before this current one, and possibly trillions before that. Ply Prism surmised this yet again. There would probably be trillions of universes after the collapse of this one, too. He had long-since suspected this, but now he somehow knew it for certain. He somehow had certainties inside. He then seemingly entered a future universe, via the ride, and via a myriad flashing lights: he'd forgotten just how disorientating this ride could be. That's if he was actually *in* the ride! Jumping heck! It was frightening. Take the biggest big-dipper ride on Earth circa 2050, then put a power sign up in the corner next to it at, say, 30. At nano-proportions, streaking along at 10-times-light-speed, the sensation was, well, other-universe. In not expecting it, Ply Prism experienced it purely. In not being prepared for it, he fell directly into it just like a child stepping off the ledge of a high building at lG on Earth.

Yet he found no initial trace of the creatures in the ride.

As a scientist, he thought, other 'superior' creatures could possibly use him as some sort of slave. They may use him in some unexpected manner. But no. Superior creatures didn't do that. It was only the *inferior* ones, he said out loud. Here he was undertaking a nano-ride which he'd not expected to do, and was now circling the canals of somebody's brain as though in a craft gliding across ancient craters somewhere - a craft that had a lot on its robotic mind. Notions of superior and inferior were now the least of his worries: he'd stepped away from himself!

And it was probably just as well.

Outside Zoe Halloway and her two children had been left alone as it were in the pleasure-dome. They watched with amazement human-species attain *pleasure* in ways which certainly she had never witnessed before. And that music. What was it?

Inadvertently, Ply Prism was also attaining pleasure - albeit at his heart's sudden expense. What Zoe Halloway witnessed in the dome was different to what Favolans witnessed there. Her Earth's perception could not conceive of Favola's parallel dimensions, hence how she and her children appeared to everyone. Also, she could not actually adjust to the dimensions, and never would. Indeed, she couldn't even see them! No. She couldn't look upon the interior of Favola as the inhabitants could, and never would. It was *different* to her than it was to them. What she saw and felt was not what the inhabitants of Favola saw and felt. Consequently, the *pleasures* of the pleasure-dome were experienced differently. Not that she'd been experiencing much. But just being there was not the same. She wasn't getting any pleasure from the pleasure-dome, she saw. It was a different atmosphere *to* pleasure.

Being millions of light-years from home didn't help, either.

"Excuse me," said a primed member of the maintenance-species, with his eighteen fingers and big crevice-searching eyes, "are you having a good time? You look a little, er, agitated. Are you all right?" He gazed down at Zoe's children as though watching a hole form. Yes, at close quarters they disconcerted him. In fact they shocked him. He'd never seen anything like them before, even in electronic-books! It seemed as though they'd been injured or something, with those angled heads and multi-twisted bodies. He felt concerned, as though they might be in pain. He genuinely wanted to help, if he could. The music echoed eerily, seemingly ghostifying to him what was now alien creatures standing directly before him. He kept his composure, though.

"Mummy, that man's got lots of fingers!" Clarest calmly declared.

"Yes, erm. We're from Earth. Have you been told about us?" Zoe too noticed the eighteen fingers on his wide hands, but then ignored them. She smiled and tilted her (to his perception) many-sided head. He blinked heavily to take it all in, she saw.

He then averted his gaze. "We all have! That's why I came up to you. I hope you don't mind. The overseers have asked us all to be as helpful as possible to you and your children. Everyone knows you're here! We have never met anybody from Earth. Do all earthlings have this appearance?"

"Well, to us *you* look strange! On Earth we probably wouldn't have the appearance you're talking about. On Earth we would look like everybody else. But that's probably of little use to you. Everyone, you say? How many people - er, sorry - human-species is that?"

"It fluctuates. Favola's 91 vicinities each have the capacity for a thousand inhabitants at any one time. So, including the children, about 100,000? It's something like that. You'll have to ask Corda for the precise figure. There are a lot of us, but only a few of us are being made regularly. We all have tasks to do. We all have leisure-time as well. But no one goes hungry or anything like that, as we've been taught other intelligent life-forms do on *many* planets. We don't really know what hunger is, in fact. But we are taught about it as children - as well and other things." Then he felt the need to say, "Are you aware that you have a multi-sided appearance to us? It's quite spectacular to look at. Very unusual. I hope you don't mind me saying." He gave her a good look - all around. "Hmmm. I've never seen anything like it before! I'd like to see what you look like on Earth. I mean, does everybody have multi-sided faces on Earth? You say you look like everybody else? It is… very unusual, as I say." The maintenance-species' callous naivity somehow suited his big, seemingly senseless eyes, as he scratched his pointed chin with three fingers from the right hand, leaving the other fifteen to hang limply in the fluffy air.

His approach, though, made her feel somewhat relaxed - if not a little concerned for how she and her children must look. She felt her face. It felt the same as it had always done. That is, three-dimensional. Multi-sided? How could that be? What must I look like, she thought! "Have you seen our guide, Ply Prism?" she then asked, now conscious of her appearance thanks to this delivered insensitivity. "He was here a moment ago." She blushed slightly, then burped again.

"I saw him step through that door there, the Nano-Prop-Virtual-Ride door. But he hasn't come out yet. That's a good ride. You should try it. Are you, ah, missing him?"

"I don't know. I don't know why he went in. He didn't say anything."

"Ply Prism is a very great scientist."

"I'm sure he is." Then she said, "Let me ask you, how do we look when we move around? Do our sides alter in the light, or darken in the shade?" She moved from light to an area of lesser light, away from her daughter, who said, Mummy, with some distress. "You see, on Earth I look a bit like you do. I don't have all these sides you talk about. It must be because we're here, on Favola. That's… very interesting." Again she felt her face. "Yes," Zoe scientifically added, "it must be because of your altered dimension. That's all it can be. This craft is in a different dimension to Earth's, isn't it."

Favola was a relativistic spacecraft, in that, being multigenerational, it was created for the myriad on-going inhabitants, who would be the only ones to perceive the universe in their particular manner. In short, it was relative only to them. Zoe Halloway had stumbled onto something that, strictly speaking, she shouldn't have stumbled onto. To have an earthling come and stay was never part of the plan. Too much time would elapse on Earth for even their grandchildren to survive Favola's hyperspace journeys, as has been said. The universe itself could only ever be accessible to those who ventured *into* it: the designers of Favola knew this.

Indeed the beings from whichever planet its astronauts left behind would never truly know about the universe. One needed to go there oneself. And so, With Zoe Halloway in such a unique situation now, it was all beginning to sink in. She was getting *accessibility* to something which she knew was never meant to be accessible to her: namely, the Cosmos in all its weird glory!

"I believe it is," the maintenance-species replied. "Favola is constructed out of exotic alloys which enable it to shift locations in the universe. That must be the cause of it!"

'I'm finding it disconcerting to imagine how I must look!" Zoe then said. Yet, when she glanced down at her feet, as now, they were planted solidly on something firm as they always were. Everything on her body still appeared the same to her. It was still *her* standing-walking-talking-sitting. It was just that, well, this *her* was not where it should have been. This *her* had been taken out of its time and place, as though death had raised it to another time and place! No, Zoe Halloway, Clarest, and Zen, who had been having mild headaches where his tumour had been removed, were no longer alive and breathing on Earth. They were instead alive and breathing millions of light-years away from Earth. They were, for all intent and purposes, dead. They had been vanished from the planet.

"It is one of the most amazing things I have ever seen in my life!" the maintenance-species commented, before tearing his eyes away to watch a gliding, grinning doctor.

Meanwhile, Ply Prism had entered holographic dimension number 30, and was delirious in it. Or, his mind was. His matter was elsewhere, in another lower-down dimension. One of the physical ones. For Ply Prism's matter had been removed from the mind that was possibly "him," which had taken itself off for a vacation without his consent, while somehow dragging the consciousness along with it just for the sake of reality - if indeed the consciousness ultimately constituted reality. Was that possible? Yes - in dimension 30! There, if indeed it *was* a 'there', mind-bending colours spoke.

And so, within the Nano-Prop-Virtual-Ride in one of Favola's great pleasure-domes, Ply Prism then made contact with the 10-dimensional ethereal beings, who had engineered it so.

His mind, or his consciousness, now spoke for itself - seemingly freed from its flesh. It didn't have much to say, but it spoke - albeit in a nervous kind of shuddering manner. "Who, who are you?" it said. There was no sound, just the notion of the question in a bundle of thought. The light around it was very strong. Or, it would have been to Ply Prism's eyes - had they been experiencing light. It was just his mind. His mind - now heightened - saw this strong light, but did not blink. For the mind didn't require sunglasses. The mind could gaze directly at light and not squint, even when the light was as bright as this. Yes, the mind had eyes; it was just that, with the universe only looking as it did to human beings, and then as it did to Favolans, the eyes which the mind used could not be seen with conventional eyes, as it were. The mind's eyes were *invisible.*

"You know who we are," came an answer. "You have always known."

Ply Prism's invisibility had him at a loss. He felt abstracted in the extreme. "The Cosmos?" he asked, not knowing why.

"You have always known the answer to that as well," said the voice.

"I have?" Before he could metaphorically blink, Ply Prism's mind now instantly found itself encased in flesh again. The body which worked for it came to with great aches and groans outside the ride. But he didn't want to be in flesh again, he saw. He was just getting the hang of *not* being in flesh. It was very interesting, too. His body, in a sense, had in fact briefly died - and Corda had registered this from Favola. But now, he was outside the door to the ride, alive again, and being helped to his quivering feet by the maintenance-species known as Clung Overloop, as well as Zoe Halloway. His face wore an expression of, it seemed to her, abject wonderment. He even looked ecstatic.

"What happened to you?" she asked as her children also gathered round in a confused sensation of being somewhere… very strange.

He was speechless. "I… I… made contact."

"Are you all right now?" asked the ever-insensitive Clung Overloop. "Because, er, I have to get back to my post. Pleasure over for one day!" He sort of nervously laughed at Zoe's multi-sidedness.

"Yes, yes, I'm fine." Ply Prism waved him away as he got to his feet. Then, in Clung Overloop's absence, he said, "Zoe, I made contact with the aliens! I must inform the captain. It was amazing. They are… beautiful! I had a sense of knowing much more than I could ever know while in this body! They took me *out* of my body! It was a wonderful feeling." He looked back towards the door. "I want to be with them again! I… know them!"

"Ply, get a grip!" said Zoe, gripping his arm. "You're a scientist…"

"They've captured… so much… energy…"

At that moment the captain and two officers appeared in the dome and came to see if Ply Prism was really dead. As far as he was concerned Ply Prism had just been registered as *ceasing to exist.* It was good to see that the opposite was the case.

Peeler Curvature embraced him.

"Captain," the living Prism then gasped, "I made contact with the intruders!"

CHAPTER NINE

CORDA HAD BEEN OBSERVING spectacular gamma-ray bursts from the bridge in their new location in the universe. They were being recorded in Vicinity 20, too, emanating from a distant, fading black hole. It was an interesting spectacle, Corda was interested to behold. They didn't last long, however. Just the odd recorded light-speed purple flash. That was all. But the power behind them was almost that of a few harnessed stars: Favola had recorded this. They illuminated the bridge as a nuclear weapon might illuminate a human brain…

It should be said that the bridge to Favola had something of a 21st Century Earth's luxury liner's feel to it, only infinitely more advanced. While one of Earth's luxury-liner bridges was sprawling in its vision of great blue oceans, Favola's was breath-taking in its magnificent panorama of outer-space - to Zoe Halloway's perception. Although, as has been said, her view was not that of Favolans. But even to them the panorama was an amazing one, when viewed from the trans-core viewing-screen that stretched *around* the bridge in one span. And Favola's actual size, too. That needed to be comprehended by a human mind. On Earth, or, more specifically, the North Wales coast of the British Isles on Earth, to use an analogy, Favola was about the size of the island of Anglesey - only perfectly circular. From a vantage-point in space it would appear as flat because of this size, but was in fact about 150 metres deep. If Favola ever *did* land on Earth, it would seem as though a piece of the land had taken flight into the sky. For it would create a shadow over any valley, and would look like a moon while higher up in the cool atmosphere. It would also probably cause weather disruption where there hadn't been any for centuries. Indeed, Favola's size would be hazed-out by Earth's atmosphere if it ever landed there - even on a clear day. For if a human being stood on a rim of the great craft they would be hard-pushed to view the *opposite* rim!

The captain and the two officers calmly entered the bridge once again.

"Sir, we are getting a reading of the 10-dimensional beings in Vicinity 20," Corda immediately informed him before he had time to think. He then briefly watched the gamma-ray bursts as Corda spoke. "Favola informs me that they are in fact standing - if that's what they do, Sir - in front of the cone-screens - viewing them, it would appear. Should we take any action?"

Peeler Curvature moved to his post and squinted at the gamma-ray bursts, which then stopped. He observed the blackness of space momentarily, then looked to Xenon Ream, who was seated behind him - now recovered from his minor upset. "Corda, Ply Prism did not cease to exist! He still exists. He made contact with the intruders. That somehow gave the reading of his demise. We do not know what happened to him. The only thing he can recall is an intense light, and a massive sensation of, as he says, well-being." Peeler Curvature gazed behind at the overseer. "He says that he gained an understanding of the universe, Xenon, beyond which even Favola does not have! I do not know what he means…"

"Quite, captain," said Corda in front of him.

"As a scientist we must respect his knowledge and what he says," Xenon Ream then commented. "I have known Ply Prism for over a century. I know that he showed great intelligence as a youth. He is not known for his exaggerations. There must be a reason why the intruders chose him to communicate with. Ply Prism had 36 brothers and 29 sisters - all brought up from the Tube in a similar way, and I've known them all. Ply had something special, it seemed to me. We will respect what he has to tell us of his findings." He waved a long hand from the rear of the bridge, as though covering the viewing-screen with invisible silk.

"If these intruders are as fantastic as Ply Prism says," said the captain, "then they should have no problem getting back to their galaxy from wherever we drop them off! And I intend to do that soon. Xenon, we cannot have univited guests on Favola - wonderful as they might be!"

"This is true," gasped Xenon Ream, nodding. "This is very true."

Back at the pleasure-dome Zoe and Ply Prism were taking refreshments, while her two children played in a large virtual chamber. Clarest and Zen were space-walking on the surface of Favola - without space-suits - in complete safety. The whole of the cosmos was visible to them, as they laughed and leapt and somersaulted in an echoing silence, then flew into the echo *of* this silence. Great stars were as bright as domestic lights at home to them, and there were thousands of them all around, just floating. Clarest and Zen didn't know where they were, nor even what stars were; yet their voices reverberated in the humming void: the virtual chamber itself providing a detailed picture of walking on Favola's glimmering surface to them. To the children it was a magical, safe experience.

"I find this music intriguing, Ply," said Zoe Halloway as she sipped liquid in a type of cafe environment, surrounded by a number of other inhabitants, drinking too. "I can truly say that I've never heard anything like it before! It's so… strange!" The liquid was thickish, and blue in colour. Certainly the apperance wasn't appetizing; the taste, though, was - like most ingestible things on Favola, it seemed to Zoe - sweet. A blue-sweet flavour, she thought. She found it actually almost intoxicating. For it seemed to massage her throat as it went down, pulsating into her stomach in a mellow feel.

"The music is composed by Favola itself," said

Ply, sipping the same liquid. "It's structure is a condensed chromaticism within Favola's unique mode of microtones, where, as you can hear, Favola has not only used quarter tones, but sixteenth tones. Combine that with a lightly-touched polyphony, played quietly, which in itself engenders that sweet polytonality you can now hear, and what you have is Favola's actual thought-pattern in sound. In fact, the music is Favola's brain at work! To us, though, it is very reassuring. Indeed, it is the sound of home! That's how we view it."

"I can see how you feel it is beautiful. I can't feel that myself, but I can see how you might feel it." Zoe listened to the music seriously for a moment, but could not identify the sixteenth-tones. Too small a sound. It would have put modern classical composers from even the 25th century in the shade, she felt. It was very brilliant music. Difficult. Un-Earthlike. Ethereal…

"Favola's music is the only music we have!" Ply Prism then declared.

"I suppose… you don't… need any other. It's mesmerizing."

A pale green ambience then appeared to fall across the cafe, as they listened. They both sat sipping this thick liquid, feeling seemingly very good: the drink known on Favola as *Crotales*. The ambience, or lighting, seemed then to deepen. Then the most astonishing thing happened. It was something which Favola did spontaneously every so often, but only in the pleasure-domes. The section of space where the craft was located, in the galaxy JX99, now opened up to the viewers in the cafe before their eyes. Zoe and Ply, as well as all the other human-species *in* the dome, were, for all intent and purpose, in *outer-space.* Favola made itself invisible to them, so that they were sitting out there, in the universe, with not even a table! This only ever happened on occasion - possibly because of the music - and always without warning. But what a show. What a glorious, powerful drama!

The cosmos engulfed Zoe Halloway, like it never could on Earth. She momentarily panicked: lost in an alien, dreamy universe!

"It's all right," said Ply, monitoring her multi-sided expressions with something close to affection. "You are safe. Nothing has happened to Favola. It has just allowed the universe *in.* See? Aren't the stars magnificent? No one who has ventured in the cosmos could fail to be overwhelmed by the spectacle. We are, ultimately, children of the stars!" He watched it all with an unusually big smile.

Zoe went to hold the rim of her seat, but it wasn't there. Nothing from the inside was. In all actuality she appeared to be floating in outer-space. Yet she knew she hadn't been ejected from Favola because (a) she could still breathe, and (b) she hadn't exploded. So, yes, she was fine. Sort of. But, the sudden sensation was, like everything else on Favola, it seemed, disorentating. Then she calmed, saying: "That is… amazing!" Are we outside?" She glanced behind to see if anything was there.

"No. Favola has made herself invisible to us. It's a trick - Favola's little game. I love it. Don't be afraid, Zoe. Each region of space has its own illuminated structure. Each region is different."

"It's truly fantastic! I'm space-walking! I never knew… I'd… it's-" She drank some more, intoxicated even further…

"Clarest and Zen are still in the virtual chamber," Ply Prism then reassured her. "They are safe. Favola would never do anything to harm anyone. Observe: the cosmos!" He held out his arms.

Zoe then thought about her children, but in Clarest and Zen's quantum VR wildness they could suddenly somehow see their mother sitting in outer-space. They called to her, but got no reply. So, instead, they went on floating and flying. A wave from the mother would have been nice, though. Zen was a bit unhappy about that. But from Zoe's perspective, the children could not be seen. Favola hadn't needed her to see them…

"How long does it last for? I'm beginning to feel a little queasy out here. It's so… dark. Yet the light is so… intense. Starlight outside an atmosphere is a very wonderful phenomenon. It's like a vision I have always dreamt of, but never seen. Whenever I go to the moon, I am under cover, so the spectacle isn't truly observed. The shock of black light is utterly amazing. But here, the starlight is entirely different. It's a different intensity to our sun. I can see that. Yes, a different-" At that moment Ply Prism and Zoe Halloway were back at the refreshment arena, unharmed. It was all as it had been before. Favola had become visible again without ceremony. Aghast, Zoe now attempted to resume drinking. Perhaps it was the drink that helped the effect? Her blink-rate too had increased, she sensed.

Unfazed, Ply went to speak, but was taken instead by a definite voice in his head. It was one of his new-found 10-dimensional friends from levels in the hologram that he had not known existed.

"Ply, are you all right?" Zoe asked. "Are you unwell? Can you hear me?"

For three Earth-minutes Ply Prism sat motionless next to Zoe Halloway. He was clearly in a trance of some sort. Or, he was transfixed. Yet when he came out he seemed very happy. He seemed *other-worldly* happy. "I have just been given some information which Corda and the captain need to hear," he then panted. "I cannot believe the calculations that have just been made and rendered to me! They are 28-dimensional calculations, I believe. I'm afraid I must leave you for the time being, Zoe. I will tell you all once I've spoken to the captain. Please, enjoy whatever else you choose to go in." He stood lithely from the table and appeared most distracted.

"Ply, what is it? No. Don't go. I feel uneasy here alone."

He gazed down at her. "You'll be all right. Please, go and join Clarest and Zen in the main virtual chamber. Have a space-walk with them. You must experience as much as you can while you're here. You can also programme the float-car to take you to a forest. You must see the forests, Zoe. They are quite tranquil. I have to leave now. Forgive me." And he left.

Zoe gazed around the pleasure-dome in his fading absence, and felt oddly distracted. She wasn't being stared at as such; however, there was a sense of human-species catching a glimpse of her whenever she looked the other way: of turning their weird heads when she turned her equally weird head. She saw them turning *their* heads back at the precise second!

Or so it seemed. She was feeling self-conscious.

"Tranquil?" she whispered. "Everything's tranquil here," she gasped. "Children," she then said out loud as though ignoring something, "shall we go for a ride?"

CHAPTER TEN

ZOE AND THE CHILDREN accidentally rode the float-car to Vicinity 20. It wasn't intended - at least not by her. Zoe had believed that she'd programmed the vehicle for one of the forests, having been shown how to; although, in all honesty, she didn't truly know *how* to programme the vehicles. Ply Prism had simply instructed her to, er, press that button there, and it would go to wherever you wanted it to via a thought-button. But apparently not. On arriving at the docking-bay to Vicinity 20 she immediately realized that she was in the wrong location. Well, at least there weren't any trees around…

Instead, the doors to Vicinity 20 were before her, as large and as grand as the doors to a great Corinthian temple on Earth, circa 0001 AD, and there was nobody around. The ambience was more eerie than anywhere else she'd been to so far. It was an ancient atmosphere, it seemed to her. It was like going inside a pyramid on Earth, or something like that. The children, however, were quite excited. To them now, it was all a great big theme park - a sealed theme-park in space.

It was all such fun! "Mummy, look at those big doors!" cried Clarest from the front of the motionless float-car, while Zen climbed hurriedly from the rear. "Can we go inside? Oh, can we? Please? What's inside, mummy? Oh, please, let's go inside and see!" The car raised very slightly as his inconsequential weight relinquished itself from the air-jets.

"Wow," gasped Zoe. "I wonder what *is* inside? I wonder what it is? Perhaps it's a relic or something from an ancient planet." Zoe too went to get out of the car. "They are so big!" she then whispered in a daunted manner. "What could they be for?" She smiled to her children.

"Mummy," murmured Clarest after a pause, "what's a relic?"

Zen was already touching the great doors - which dwarfed him as a building dwarfs a human being - before his mother could climb from the float-car that was only a few paces away. Even the docking-bay was ornate, she observed. There seemed to be what looked like gold-leaf edging everything, and carvings and statues encircling the pathway to the great doors. Wow, she said again. There certainly was something extremely special about the place, quite clearly.

The doors opened to Zen's touch. What Zoe didn't know, of course, was that she was at Vicinity 20 - right in the centre of Favola: she'd never even heard of Vicinity 20. It hadn't been mentioned to her. There was no need for her to know, for she was never meant to go there. The float-car which she'd used hadn't been programmed to take her there. Yet it *had* taken her there. It had dropped her off directly outside: Vicinity 20 - a somewhat hallowed place…

Corda on the bridge, meanwhile, now knew that she was there.

Favola had registered it. The three earthlings were now alone with the aliens, inside. Peeler Curvature was then informed, and so was Xenon Ream. Ply Prism was already en route to the bridge, so the captain immediately sent two officers to see that Zoe Halloway came to no harm…

"Has Favola uploaded her mind?" the captain tentatively asked of Corda.

"Yes, sir. Every moment, it would appear. Zoe Halloway's life is now available for viewing in Vicinity 20. However, I suspect that if she somehow sees this on the cone-screens, she might be a little… upset? I am only presuming here, captain."

"Quite, Corda. I agree. She must not be allowed to view her life - most of which she will no doubt have forgotten anyway. Our great screens should not have been made available to her. The officers must act quickly. Corda, advise them to get a hurry on!" Peeler Curvature stood captain-like on the bridge.

"… Sir, Favola informs me that there has not been sufficient time for them to arrive at Vicinity 20 before our guests. I fear we may be too late. I will ask Favola not to display any of Zoe's life on the screens - in the unlikelihood that she comprehends the display-control, that is."

Ply Prism then entered the bridge in a mild

fluster. He gesticulated that he wished to speak to the captain in his room. Xenon Ream accompanied them, and seemed to take on Prism's discomposure. For the overseer moved in a fairly ungainly manner, which was not his wont.

The captain's room was just off the bridge, and was relatively small. It had two circular viewing-screens out onto the great and passing universe, and the captain's reflection was caught on both of them as he ambled by. He then sat at his liquid-mercury desk, which had a number of onyx controls on it, while Ply Prism stood before it. Xenon Ream sat at a chair behind them both, frowning.

"Captain, the 10-dimensional beings made detailed telepathic contact with me in the pleasure-dome concerning Zoe Halloway's return to Earth! It seems they have a way for her to get back to Earth at the precise moment before she materialized on our bridge, and then for us to be in another space-location so as not to repeat the incident. They also calculated it for us to be at this particular coordination point we are now in, exactly when she enters her own Earth-time. It requires 28-dimensional calculations, however, which I'm not sure Favola is capable of. They have given me the rudiments of these calculations, which I shall treasure always, and of which I shall punch into Favola's banks immediately. Captain, I have never known calculations like them. They are… astounding! They have temporarily imprinted the main calculations in my brain, and Favola can download them from me. Why they have done this, I cannot say. But I need for them to be removed, as I cannot conceive of anything else while they are there! The calculations place Favola at a light-speed impact with that imploding planet at the precise nano-second it explodes. They assure me that we will come to no harm. The beings inform me that the energy engendered is the only possible way for Zoe to resume her life on Earth as though she had never witnessed coming here. I know it sounds enormous, captain, and even dangerous, but I think once Favola has grasped the calculations and done them for itself we will see that it is true." Ply Prism then placed a hand on his brow, though not in a painful way. "Captain," he added, slightly concerned, "they also said - and this I cannot prove - that they… er… created human-beings! That is, they created our ancestors as a scientific experiment!" He gazed down at Peeler Curvature as though looking for an answer, who had none.

"What?" panted Xenon Ream through his grey beard.

"They claim to have created human-beings," Ply repeated, turning his head, "as a scientific experiment! They felt they could divulge this information to me. Again, I don't know why."

The captain gazed up at him from his desk. "Hmmm. It requires a lot to take on board, Ply. Ten-dimensional creatures created human-beings as a scientific experiment? Favola dives at light-speed at a planet's imploding surface? Hmmm. We need more information. It could all be an elaborate ploy."

"I know, sir. But it does actually make scientific sense when you know the calculations. They are immortal, as we know, and more advanced than Earth's civilizations would probably ever be, as there isn't enough sun-time remaining for Earth to reach even as far as these creatures were millions of Earth-years ago! Even at the time of Earth's creation from its third-generation star, these creatures were a Type III civilization, harnessing the energy from the previous *two* stars, which, as we know, Earth's sun replaced. Captain, I believe they are… what human-beings used to call… God." Ply Prism then sort of looked away towards a porthole as though in a type of prayer.

"Miraculous!" Xenon Ream declared, as he often did.

"We know that there was never any such thing," the captain then said. "God never existed on Earth, nor anywhere else. Yes, everything was created, but by emerging consciousnesses."

"We have always been calculating and perceiving in the limitation of our own brains, sir, and of our human ancestors' brains. Captain, I believe them. No, I believe *in* them. There isn't a god, of course, but there could be multiple-gods! These creatures are the closest I could imagine as such!"

"This requires a lot for us to take on board," the captain repeated. "I cannot risk Favola's safety, even for our human guests. Download your brain-pattern into Favola, Ply. Let's see what you've got. Tell your friends also that I wish to meet with them..."

Meanwhile, Zoe and her two children had actually entered Vicinity 20, tentatively. Daunted, she was overly shocked at what beheld her. For the ten great oval 8-dimensional cone-screens were standing there before her like throbbing cliffs, glowing. And there, dwarfed in front of them, were the four white 10-dimensional creatures, writhing ghostlike. The children turned in on their mother, and she held them. The fun seemed here to evaporate. But then, what was suddenly displayed on the screens removed the notion she was now feeling of abject fear. It was, she was aghast to perceive, the view from her very own eyes of her very own life! It was what she had been seeing all along, on Earth.

Her husband's face came massively into view. They were on a hot beach somewhere in California. Zoe immediately recognized the location, for it was all around her, encircling her in rich sensations, moment to moment, no editing. He lowered his sunglasses and gave her a kiss in the sunshine, just how it happened, only hugely. Someone even drifted over them on a hover-belt, waving, and Zoe remembered it. It was Earth in the mid 2400s, and it was her life! But how? Who?

What? Zoe was rigid. Then the creatures came closer, and she backed away a little in amongst her VR life. The children began to whine. "We mean you no harm," said a voice in her head fairly loudly, which was not her mind speaking. There was a definite sensation of a voice, as though you heard someone calling your name across a room. "The spacecraft has uploaded your mind to date," the voice went on. "Do not be angry with it. It was acting naturally. Behold! Your life!"

Zoe blinked heavily, and that seemed to alter the era. She was now a teenager, and in a vehicle with her father. They were hovering around corners in the domed city of San Francisco, with the new bridge to their left, all under glass. She blinked again, and she was at her wedding in Italy. She was amongst it - the smells and sounds and other intense earthly sensations. But somehow it was more real than when she actually experienced it. Somehow it gave the emotion of knowing her own life in a godlike manner: of knowing it much more fully than actually living it! She blinked again, and she was 21 - riding a horse through a forest in Yellowstone. But it was all so big - so huge - those screens were enormous. The reality they created was a vast reality. It was around her. It engulfed her. Her own life!

A magnificence fell into her body via the eight dimensions. They had her immersed within the very world of themselves - of the cone screen's spectacular display - within the world she was viewing, her own world. It was literally a feeling that she had never had before, even though it was confusing. For they turned her around inside this world. They turned this world inside out for her. She felt excited, as though in a drug-induced bliss. The visions encircled her and her children, giving the impression that the entire universe was made up of only Zoe Halloway's life, and nothing else, ever. In fact her life seemed bigger *than* the universe. Already she had discovered things about herself which she had never known. Her family's bodies would move through her, around her, under her. *Inside her.* She felt their own individualised emotions. Whichever way she looked she was encircled by all aspects of her life to date - and even, if she blinked, her coming aboard Favola. But what was it for? No. She didn't even question it. It was too wonderful to question. She was a child again filled with the unquestioning wonderment of existence. And she didn't even notice the ethereal beings touching her, if it was actually a touch. They writhed in front of her, sensing the children's curious distress, but placing various positive emotions into them with the flick of a thought. To the children it was a scary grotto on the scale of a mountain. But there was nothing to fear, now. They engendered it thus.

Of the initial ten human-beings whom the ethereal creatures originally left on the planet Earth, this particular family, they knew, came from the fourth one's long lineage. The initial ten's blood could still be traced, and had been logged and documented by the rock-probe on Earth. Intricate data had been constantly beamed back to the invisible planet of the 10-dimensional creatures whom Ply Prism now believed created mankind. Although, it wasn't a planet, in the conventional, tangible sense they lived on, invisible or not. It was a hyperplanet within dark-matter's wider realm, Favola would eventually reveal. Even Favola itself was part of their design. There was nothing they didn't know about Earth and its creatures, and the entire universe. They knew everything. For they were at least three-times as old as the current universe: mankind was only a tiny part of what they did.

They knew all there could ever be to know, and could act upon it.

Now they needed to calculate a plan to survive the collapse of this universe at the Big Crunch, only to go on once more in the following one as they were already in this one: that was how they worked. This would have nothing to do with Favola, but Favola would know because the beings wished it to know. They survived from one universe to the next, while inside the Metaverse simultaneously, forever. Galaxies and solar-systems in this holographic layer were almost incidental to them, to say nothing of Black Holes. It seemed that the trick for all Type III civilizations - and there were many in the universe - was to capture as much zero-point energy and star-power as possible during the enormous lifetime of a particular universe, in order to calculate how to make the jump from crunch-ripple to bang-ripple again, without any damage. Not much of a task, really, for ones so advanced. For each crunch-ripple sent up a different set of particles, and therefore a different set of physics. New matter and energy came into being with each bang-ripple via the crunch, as well as some of the old stuff that would somehow survive the crunch, like the material known on Earth as gold, for example. These creatures truly were stars - in the cosmic, dynamic sense of the old-Earth term. Stars like movie and pop-stars in just one tiny Earth-period could never comprehend. They were the star-creatures of not just this universe, but of every universe to come. What made them? They made themselves. They made the notion of *being made.* They made the concept of consciousness as a tool which minds could use in solid dimensions, all for benign, hyper-amusement.

Hence the need to seriously play themselves.

Yet they were wholly immeasurable in their understanding…

CHAPTER ELEVEN

IT TRANSPIRED that the ten-dimensional creatures brought into being the exotic alloy known as Nebstron, which Favola was made of, and of which helped advanced Earth's civilization towards becoming a Type I…

Indeed, all the major inventions and discoveries by people across Earth's centuries - not to mention the myriad conscious creatures on all the other inhabited planets in the Milky Way - were brought into being by the creators. That is, ideas were placed in various thoughtful minds by a thought-button - thought being just that: the coming-into-being of unknown life. These minds had been chosen that way. These minds had even been made that way. These minds then sort of acted independently with the new idea in place, and unknown life welled up. Yes, all concepts on every inhabited planet in the Milky Way were brought about by the creators, even the destructive ones.

Wars, it seemed, were part of the creative, moving-on process - though not, it would appear, for the people who were killed in them. Natural disasters too, inexplicably…

When left alone with the information the creatures who had attained a level of consciousness through various evolutionary states seemingly knew that to destroy was part of the bigger picture. (It appeared to be a natural state of mind for most societies on advanced planets, the astronomer-species had themselves discovered). For the inhabitants of Earth, though, the placing of ideas often sent various human-beings insane: the names were legion…

Zoe Halloway now knew all of this too, although she couldn't comprehend it. The language being used was not simple language - how could it be? It was a highly complex report.

The creators? No. It didn't gel. The information kept coming, nonetheless.

The reasoning behind wars, it seemed, was to edge a planet into becoming a Type I civilization no matter what - that is, as acting as one cohesive globe under the one single international language and, yes, eventually caring administration. But deaths and destruction - which didn't seem to matter all that much the message was saying - were surely too much to ask just for progression? Did the end ever truly justify the means? It was the overall picture which drove them, came the response for Zoe - even though various armies and governments of the past did not always know what the overall picture was, if at all. The English language on Earth had become the international language in Zoe Halloway's day. This was true. Though it had taken an awful long time and an awful lot of effort for it to happen, English was finally deemed the most malleable tool of communication. It eventually transpired that all the other languages on Earth would be fazed out, beginning first with the minority ones. But whichever language it was, a planet needed an international one before it could even think of becoming a Type I civilization, which would then, and only then, able it to advance towards becoming a Type II, and ultimate survival. Zoe now knew this for certain - though she wasn't hearing it in words. It was survival of the species that was, paradoxically, the driving-force behind all wars, even if it was only a subliminal driving-force…

The 10-dimensional, immortal beings told her that the death and destruction brought about by wars also engendered techniques for ultimate survival. Consequently, after all its many wars, Earth, by the year 3457, was on its way to truly becoming a Type II civilization, another two centuries off or thereabouts. The Sun's energy would be wholly harnessed and its power would be perfectly under humanity's control, even though it only had some 5-billion years of life remaining. It would swell, shrink, then either die or explode, only to be replaced by a new star in the same spot - a transition which, hopefully, humanity would be able to surmount. That star, then, would be the last one to sit at that space-coordination point before the universe entered the Big Crunch. But, alas, as has been said, Earth would be wiped out long before it ever became a Type III civilization, long before the Big Crunch. So, perhaps it wouldn't make the transition from star to star after all. For even the creators didn't know the future, they said. And yet, they could go there? They could go to the future. So, were they even being playful in their information? Also, Zoe asked herself, could an immortal being be cognizant of a mortal's anxieties?

Unlikely. Zoe was then given more information, whether she liked it or not. She was told that each and every single entity who was killed in any war situation, and on any planet, was later reborn into the same entity at some later stage in that planet's history. Yes, *rebirth.* As a gift these entities would be the only ones to have a tangible memory of their first existence - no matter how brief - and devoid of any emotion concerning it. It was a kind of reward, or a type of compensation. A compensation for not being allowed a life for the sake of the planet's moving-on, for the sake of the planet's progression. (These were Zoe's words. Words laid down and how her brain interpreted the information which the 10-dimensional creatures were giving her). So, maybe the creators were, after all, cognizant of a mortal's painful anxieties. For rewards spoke of a knowledge of some wrong-doing and/or gifts for work carried out. They had been put into place for centuries on Earth.

Enlightenment moved in mysterious ways.

And even as the officers arrived at Vicinity 20's docking bay, the information kept on coming. But

Zoe was now so absorbed in her own massive existence that the complexity was becoming rebuffed and eventually confused. Outside this world, though, the officers were denied entry. Vicinity 20 was closed to them. Beyond the great doors the marvel of what Zoe Halloway was experiencing and feeling was so intense, so fantastic, so *beautiful,* that she had seemingly been removed from the actual existence which was her 'real' corporeal fleshy life!

Corda attempted to open the doors from the bridge, but Favola said no. Then Zoe's life was suddenly removed from the cone-screens, and she fell to her knees. At this stage the children were weeping, but as the officers were then allowed access to the hallowed arena, and came rushing in, they calmed a little. The officers dashed directly to the children, and immediately picked them up. Zoe gazed up at them from her knees. She was semi-delirious, and had no real idea of what had just taken place. The 10-dimensional beings instantly left the vicinity. A male officer then helped Zoe to her feet, while holding Zen in his arms.

"Maddam, we had orders to attend to you. Are you all right? Are your children all right?" The officer who spoke then looked into Zen's multi-sided face and frowned as if attempting to focus. He hadn't been this close to the humans before, nor to any human, for that matter. Zen's eyes had him at a loss. For they too appeared to be, on closer inspection, bi-spherical. "The captain said that we should, ah, take you back to your chalet," he then added, mumbling it. "You were not supposed to come here. You're not supposed to be here. Vicinity 20 is a hallowed place for us." He looked to his female associate for confirmation of this.

"I didn't do it intentionally," Zoe croaked.

"Yes," the female officer confirmed, holding Clarest, "even we can only come here when we are chosen. The captain and the overseers are the only ones who may enter at will!"

"Look, I just said I didn't do it intentionally! What… is this place? Vicinty 20? What's it all about? I… I… saw my life, unfolding. Things I'd forgotten. What's going on?" She staggered a little as she stood, dizzy. "How do you people know about my life!" she managed to yell.

"We do not, maddam," the third officer then responded. "Favola does."

Back in the captain's room Ply Prism was still expanding on the 10-dimensional communication he'd had. The worlds within worlds theory had taken on a new meaning for him. The information *he* received had placed the minute electron at a million times larger than something called the *Glus,* which dwelt in a realm so small that atoms appeared as actual planets to it, with atmospheres; yet conscious creatures subsisted on spherical surfaces there, where, way down beyond the Plank level, they lived out meaningful existences, and had acquired the knowledge of space-travel. Needless to say the 10-dimensional creatures could visit, and did often, usually for drinks and nibbles, though they had no probes there. Nonetheless, they influenced every invention and progression with their thought-buttons down on Glus-globes, but were only 'creators' in their own Milky Way. Other types of 10-dimensional creatures ran other galaxies, and had their own playful information to part.

"Captain, when Favola downloads what I have in my brain it may take some time to assimilate the overall information. I estimate about 7-Earth years. But we will all be transformed by what transpires. Sir, I believe Favola will grow from it. A total assessment of the universe will then be required by us."

"Hmmm. Is that the way you see it, Ply?" Xenon Ream kindly asked.

"It is, Xenon. However, the initial information should only take a matter of minutes for Favola to incorporate. She too will then see that what the beings propose is the only possible way to get Zoe Halloway back to her original time-fabric, with no harm done. I believe we must act, captain."

"If this is so, then I agree. Very well. Begin the downloading-process. The quicker I can comprehend what is being proposed the quicker we can act on it. Ply, are you sure you are happy with this? You know that it is a voluntary act. I cannot command you to give up what you say you now have in your head, nor would I. There must be a reason why the beings chose you to make contact. We are deeply curious, however, as to what is there, and as to what may happen. Xenon, do you agree that he should allow Favola to download this information?"

"Only if Ply himself is comfortable with it, yes."

"I am, sir. I believe it has to be done."

"Then bring it into being," the captain charged. "The sooner the better."

Meanwhile, Zoe and her children were taken back to the guest chalets in the officer's float-car, where she had fallen asleep from seeming exhaustion. However, she did not dream her normal sort of dreams. That is, while catnapping, Zoe would have vivid visions of all the things in her life, from her family to her colleagues to her home. Here, the visions were highly tangible, and not related. But then she wasn't really catnapping. As she had been away from Earth for some 50-Earth minutes at this stage - although not always travelling in hyperspace and beyond-light-speed - probably some 30 years had elapsed back home. She now somehow knew this for certain. She now had a real sense of how much older than her her husband must be. In fact, she actually saw him in her mind. He was in his 80s, she saw. She also had a sense that, if she perhaps stayed aboard Favola for many years - as indeed she was now beginning to wish for - and was then dropped off back on Earth, she would be way, way into the future, way beyond her own time. Say, two or even three thousands years hence!

Imagine it? she imagined, imagining it.

The hyper-physics of her situation had been made clear in her mind, and had come into play there: she now knew them. Or, she imagined she did. As she dozed she was adding up. No, she was multiplying. No, she was calculating! It was all becoming clear to her now. Her brain was able to take it in. For wasn't this also part of the bigger plan? She was beginning to believe it was. To have her taken from her own time, and placed back on her planet at a much later date? Perhaps, she dreamily mused, they had something in mind for her? Perhaps she was to be some sort of link with Earth's past, when earthlings of the future had long forgotten it? Yes, it was all pre-ordained, and she had been chosen as some sort of space-guru, with extraordinary knowledge to help Earth's future stricken population combat a future dwindling sun, or something. Well, why not? Or, perhaps it wasn't ordained, but the creators needed certain beings along the way to put things right, to help keep it all going as they wanted it to go, she imagined, until the end. The End, as in Big Crunch. No, that didn't seem right. Too much could go wrong before The Big Crunch, if indeed there was *to be* a big crunch! The calculations were actually coming to philosophical conclusions for her. It was remarkable. How could calculations do that? The conclusions weren't always correct, but the fun was in doing them. Yes, Zoe Halloway had a taste of how *play* felt to a superior being. Gosh. She even gulped at the thought of it, at the thought of actually thinking *superior being*. It just wasn't done on Earth, and hadn't been for centuries. On Earth it was illegal to say that someone was different to someone else. You'd get fined for that. You'd lose use of the Transdoor for a whole month! And to say that *superior beings* did nothing but play? Gosh. One would be banished to the lunar mining colonies for a whole century!

CHAPTER TWELVE

INCONGRUOUS THINGS were now happening on Favola. Corda had been constantly checking the computer banks for malfunctions: there weren't any.

While Ply Prism was having his brain downloaded in a cerebral clinic in Vicinity 35, the 10-dimensional creatures extracted Zoe and her children to a fairly remote forest on one of Favola's outer rims - close to the astronomer-species. The children had been playing happily with the float-belts in their quarantined vicinity - then were standing in a silent wood, under a silent blue lighting, in silence - when in shock it happened. In less than a flash. For it happened at the speed of thought. The forest had birds in it, with the gentle sound of running water; again, Zoe Halloway was disorientated. By now, though, her disorientations were becoming so regular that she not only expected them, but would be somehow further disorentated if they didn't transpire! Disorientation was, it seemed to her by then, the norm aboard Favola. In fact she was beginning to need them: she needed to be disorentated in order to feel 'normal' on this craft, she'd been telling herself!

Not so the children.

Happy to be away from the 'funny people,' they were enjoying flying around the street outside their chalet, when they were grounded, literally, on soil. On earth. And there, in the close distance, on earth also, were the writhing 10-dimensional beings - in between some old trees!

But was the earth earth, or was it something synthetic, or even alien? Well, yes. It was soil from Earth, from a thousand years ago. From Montana in North America, to be exact. It had been secretly extracted and shipped into orbit over a period of decades, as well as all of Favola's water. Rich soil. Good earth. And well-tended, too. For it was perpetual in its life-giving nutrients, this earth, even though it was on a spaceship. Understandably, Zoe felt acutely emotional when she perceived it. She even knelt to hold the stuff in her hands. Yes, it felt the same as it did back home. It felt like… soil. It felt… soily – brown and damp. It was sweet-smelling soil! How lovely. But how immortal.

"Are we back home yet, mom?" asked Zen, beginning to feel his mother's disorientated distress. But then, on seeing the creatures, he already knew the answer.

"No, darling. Not yet." She swallowed a tear.

"Mummy, the white people!" Clarest observed, pointing. "Look!" She tugged at her mother's shirt, which was tucked into a silver cylinder that covered half of her legs in the current Earth-style.

Then, as she pointed, the 10-dimensional beings were immediately before the three of them. Zoe stood as calmly she could. Then she felt calmed as before. It was like taking a pill or something. She felt nice. She just felt… calmed. Calming. A calming effect. She felt good. It was as though her and her children and been given a deep-serenity tranquillity-tablet on Earth, where, after ingestion, there was nothing *to* fear, she saw. Indeed, it was the opposite of fear: it was… joy. Zoe began to feel elated in the presence of the 10-dimensional beings. Aliens, perhaps, but more *human,* in a sense, than anyone she had ever known - including her father. They were… God, she suddenly deduced. G,G,God! The feeling was ultra-real. She and her children were in flesh, standing before God, she thought!

But that wasn't possible, was it? "It isn't possible…" she gasped.

"Mummy, I like the white people!" Clarest declared, smiling. Then she kind of ascended from the ground to about a metre, to be closer to them - at will. Clarest willed it.

Then Zen, too. He rose, was embraced, was touched - without being touched. Nonetheless, he felt reassured with this touch. This contact. He was embraced as one, by four. They touched him as one. The white people entered his mind and made it clear that they would always be there for him, as one. This they did in that forest, on the edge of the great craft Favola. They'd be there, they told him. Never - in this universe or the next - would Zen be without the 10 dimensional creatures, if he so desired. This they told him in that Favolan forest. The white people would make a separate human being out of him: they would make him unique, they told him. Zen would be, in privacy, unique. They would alter his growing understanding of the universe almost to their understanding - which was actually beyond the understanding of any human being ever, but that didn't matter, then. For Zoe cried the most intense bliss for her son at what she saw and perceived. *She saw. She felt.* Nothing on Earth could make her feel as she was feeling then. Nothing. In an instant she was feeling more elated and overwhelmed with the elation than she had ever done before. What were these creatures? Where were they from? It didn't matter. She didn't need to know. They were too beautiful to ask…

Dark-matter's energy in a zero-point field that surrounds galaxies was used specifically by them, Zen now knew. That was his first simple lesson. That, and the electrical power of stars, was what powered them. Much would follow. But that information also didn't matter. Zen was perhaps too young anyway.

Back on the bridge, Corda, experiencing an emotion close to concern, appeared not to be in control of the ship. Corda had *no* control, it was appearing!

"Sir, we are entering hyperspace without either your command or my control!" he then informed the captain, who was standing behind. "I fear that we have been, well, taken over." A flash of electronic panic ran through Corda's artificial chromosomes at that declaration, causing a cheek-twitch, which almost created imbalance within his/her personality. Corda's personality was, in a sense, decided and structured by the genetic inheritance that he/she was given by his/her creators - namely the scientists who made him/her. Consequently, Corda was phlegmatic at all times - almost. But this was one of the times when a long-gone scientist's deep-seated fears broke surface to cause that constant to become… well, slightly inconstant. This was one of the rare times in Corda's thousand-year history that a cheek-twitch indicated an ancient pre-given emotion: namely disturbance, interlaced with silly worry, which a naïve scientist many centuries ago once had and once gave.

"That can't happen, Corda," Peeler Curvature remarked. "Favola is linked directly to you. If there is a problem you naturally know about it. If we have been taken over you can take us back. Take control, Corda. That's an order!"

"I am attempting to, captain, and have been for a while now. It would appear to be impossible, however. The 10-dimensional creatures are controlling Favola through me, and there is nothing I can do about it. I would suggest that you either remove me from my post, or, I'm afraid, dismantle me. But I fear also that that will do no good. They would override those commands as well. No. We must await their desires. We are, sir, at their mercy…" Corda gazed somewhat longingly at Peeler Curvature, who stood behind in an air of indignation, in the centre of the room. It was true that Corda's inbuilt intelligence, while beyond any human intelligence, could nonetheless mimic the feelings of a human being when necessary - even showing signs of attraction to that human being, if needs be - for Corda was capable of a type of love. The personality being placed there during birth/construction by, yes, one of the initial scientists, had the capacity for it. Corda very possibly *did* love. And it was love which flowed inside then, even though danger seemed to have them all prisoner.

"There must be something we can do!" yelped the captain. "I feel we must make immediate direct contact with them. We need to see what it is they desire of us. Corda, can you locate their whereabouts? It has become imperative."

"I can, captain. They are in forest number 4, close to the Smanioso Lake - with Zoe Halloway and her children. All float-cars have been rendered out-of-action, however. As you know it is a day's walk to that location, sir. I am trying everything in my power to overcome their commands!"

"We need to be there now, Corda. Where is that diamond-probe of theirs? They must know that I need to speak with them!"

"I fear they do, sir. However, your wishes appear, well, irrelevant to them…"

In Vicinity 35 Ply Prism had finished having the

information downloaded into Favola's computer banks, as indeed the 10-dimensional creatures intended - which was a fairly simple process anyway. He felt oddly light-headed after it, though. One probe was required to be attached to his brow. That was all. It took moments for the downloading process to take place, and the information was then immediately relayed to the bridge, where Corda translated it. However, as the downloading took place while Favola was actually in hyperspace, the readings and computations appeared augmented - as indeed the 10-dimensional creatures had intended. It was as though, revealing them *within* hyperspace, somehow completed them. The motion and expansion of hyperspace stretched out the calculations to fulfil even *their* tremendous cosmological computations, still further.

"Sir," Corda then calmly informed Peeler Curvature, who was making ear-piece contact with as many officers as possible, themselves close enough to the forest to get there on foot, albeit not very soon, "the information from Ply Prism's brain is now available for us. It is… astonishing, captain. But I am perplexed as to why we haven't discovered these calculations ourselves before. They seem so… simple! They are, I believe, within our grasp. However, as they are in the field of 28-dimensional calculation - simple once that itself has been realized - it is possible that only a handful of human beings in any one epoch on Earth could comprehend them. Fortunately, you are human-species, and I believe that many inhabitants will comprehend what is being suggested here, as I myself already have. Sir, you must now look for yourself!" Corda leaned back as Peeler Curvature leant forward…

… Stunned. "I see," he gasped. "Yes. I see! That infinite dark-matter trajectory will place Zoe and her children in the circular sphere of ten-to-the-power-eighteen orbital transcendental, precisely where she needs to be. Absolutely remarkable. Why couldn't we have come up with this, Corda? Why couldn't Favola! The linear-curvature is, if I'm not mistaken, an electron-thrust of eighteen-to-the-power-thirty-eight stroke nine-latch-forty-one-distant, which then closes over spacetime's hydrogen-gap of chaotic gravity. Yes, I see. This is truly spectacular! These numbers are so outlandish, so meticulous, that a nano-hair couldn't fit between them! Corda, the astronomer-species will now have to alter their entire lexicon. All their globes will be out of place within their constructed universe." He gazed on, marvelling at the calculations as they became even clearer.

"Sir, I believe the aliens aboard wish us no harm. Indeed, Favola informs me that she senses they wish us well. Furthermore, we get a feeling that they have - and I have no proof of this – been with us always. We are now getting a sense of how we believe they are, captain. It is as though Favola herself has allowed me into her very core and given me the secrets of all the previous universes to this current one, via our 10-dimensional friends. I am, sir… in coition - if that is the correct terminolgy." Corda even felt a tinge of, as perceived, mild embarrassment.

"We, Corda?" asked the captain.

"Yes, sir. Favola and I are currently acting as one entity. We are… *we!*"

"… And what else are you both currently experiencing?"

Corda fell momentarily silent, as new data came through, because Favola was now at the exact same coordination point which it was previously at, close to the imploding planet in the twin system. It had got there via a thought-window, which Favola didn't even know existed, but could only be instigated by Type III civilizations. "Sir, we have now re-located to the imploding planet. Observe. I believe we have been perfectly aligned for the light-speed shoot. It is… quite remarkable, in my opinion." Corda gazed out at the spectacular sight. It appeared as though the planet was on the point of critical collapse, with much electromagnetic energy recorded. There was a display of purple lightning flashes and greenish haloes, combined with blue-gold gravity bursts firing around the neutron star.

"No order has been given for that location!" the captain snarled. "Corda, inform our guests that I demand to speak with them immediately!"

CHAPTER THIRTEEN

THE ASTRONOMER-SPECIES informed Peeler Curvature that a rare alloy had been located on a different, more stable planet in the same solar-system - a system which Favola had no intention of ever returning to, but which was now encircling the great craft in a silent motion.

With this information, and with Captain Curvature aware of how important the rare alloy was to them, (they'd been searching for it for some two-hundred years, and were keen to experiment with it in some capacity) he wanted to send an investigative team down to the surface in an Alternative Craft. The discovery of this alloy - a substance that could make invisible anything which was constructed out of it, as had been demonstrated by a highly advanced Type II civilization in the J250 galaxy - was to the captain every bit as important as getting Zoe and her children home precisely. But then, as he gave new orders to Corda concerning who should go down to the planet, he instantly materialized in the forest, directly *next* to Zoe Halloway. Who, it has to be said, let out a quiet yell at the extra sudden vision. And a jump, too. But that was okay. *It* was okay. The 10-dimensional creature's other-dimensionness held her mind in an invisibly caressing cradle-motion, she mused. In fact she was wholly caressed by them. One could have even said *drugged.* And Zen, too. He also was held. He also was caressed. But not Clarest. She, it seemed, was too young. Maybe their caressing wouldn't have had an effect on her mind: she was happy, nevertheless. Happy to see mummy happy.

"What is going on?" Peeler Curvature immediately asked, not in the least bit fazed. "You are running Favola," he said directly to the creatures in the serene forest. "You have not been invited to run Favola. I am asking you to desist from doing that! Desist from running Favola!" As he spoke, the creatures moved, and both Peeler and Zoe then found themselves on the surface of the planet, seemingly, where the rare alloy was to be found. But no. It was in fact Earth – circa, 1670.

"I can breathe!" Zoe declared, as though she couldn't before. Glancing around, she was in further shock, and no longer calmed. The scenery looked familiar enough - if not a little overgrown and wild. But the silence. The silence was other-worldly. The silence was not of any world *she* knew. Yet it was her world. It was, she felt, Earth. Europe. Possibly France. Neither knew where they were, nor why. "What has happened to us?" Zoe seriously asked the captain. "Where are my children! Where are *we!*"

Peeler Curvature grasped inside his pocket for a tiny device. He held it up and looked at it. "Favola is not in the immediate vicinity," he then said very clinically. "At first I thought we'd been sent to the planet where the rare alloy was. Now I'm not so sure. I do not believe this is such."

"What rare alloy?"

"That planet has only a thin atmosphere," he went on.

"Which planet?"

"Later, Zoe. Here, although the air tastes somewhat sweet and moist, we can breathe perfectly normally. How very odd. How very odd indeed." He gazed around at his new, somewhat beautiful surroundings in a curious air. The trees and earth struck him as quite lovely. The light, too. It was so rich. "Are you okay, er, Zoe?" He looked to her, before attempting ear-implant communication with Corda. He then awaited Zoe's response thoughtfully, but none transpired. They were, it seemed, alone. But alone where? And through which mode of transportation? 'Earth, said a voice in simultaneous ears. You are on Earth in Earth's mid-to-late Seventeenth Century. You are in the country known as France, the reason for which will be made clear to you.' The voice then stopped.

There was a huge silence.

"I'm all right," Zoe eventually responded, no longer multi-sided, yet shaken. "What happened? What's going on?" Their voices resounded in the huge silence, a silence that was too big to be anything after Earth's Industrial Revolution, a silence from a time long before any jet-aged human beings had emerged.

"I don't know," said Curvature honestly, checking every instrument he had on his person, then trying again with his ear-implant. "Did you hear that voice? It said… Earth?"

"I heard it. Look at that sky. Look how bright it is. Look at these fields, these trees - those birds! It *is* Earth! But… how? And where are my children!" Then Zoe experienced that intense calmness again, and she knew because of it that her children were safe. They were all right. The calmness was a very tangible sensation. She now somehow grasped what it meant: it meant love…

And Peeler Curvature, too. He experienced the calmness - though in a different way to Zoe's as he had a different physicality. But it was nonetheless 'calming' - this feeling, this sensation. "Earth!" he then gasped in curious wonderment. "It is… beautiful! So… real! How can I ever go back to Favola after this, he wistfully declared!" His mind had seemingly suddenly been literally opened to all sorts of possibilities, and it felt wonderful. It felt exciting - if not a little overwhelming. *He* felt wonderful, and, how could he put it, *free!* Yes, free! He felt free for possibly the first time in his long life. "Free-dom?" he quietly emphasized, gazing around at ancient French countryside in a type of longing admiration. For he was completely humbled by his ultra-real location. In fact there wasn't any doubt about it: he was in France!

"The smells," Zoe whispered. "The light. The silence. The… warmth? Our sun is so lovely. I'd never really seen it before. Oh, I'd seen it. But I hadn't *seen* it. It's such a life-giving orb!

What had come over them? Where had the scientific reasoning and rationalization gone? "I have never experienced this," the then star-struck Peeler Curvature ranted. "We've been to the surface of many planets - lots with advanced life - but none like this. This warmth is so… perfect. *It* is so perfect. It is… home! I don't see why Favola cannot come to this place, this time-fabric, and we can all dwell in this country! It can be done, I'm sure of it! We can do it!" At that point Corda finally made contact with the captain. His quaint trance, or heightened-awareness state, to be kind, seemed to lift.

"Sir, we have located yours and Zoe Halloway's position. You are within Favola's scanning rim, but in another time-fabric altogether. Or so it would appear. You are on Earth, it seems, yet Earth some two-thousand years ago from our almanac. It appears, sir, that the earth was in this location at that period of the universe. Can you hear me, sir? Captain, are you there?"

…"Yes Corda. Perfectly, now. Can you get us back to the ship?"

"How are my children?" Zoe shouted at Peeler Curvature.

"Fine, madam. I'm not entirely sure that I can, sir. I cannot as yet, anyway. But we are working on it. I have located the hole in the time-fabric which you and Zoe Halloway seemed to have fallen through. Are you in any danger'?"

"No, Corda. Not immediately anyway. However, we will need to return to our own time before things begin going awry - as they do in misplaced time-fabric…"

"Quite, sir." Then Corda was cut off. "Get us home, Corda!" Zoe yelled.

Peeler Curvature appeared highly concerned for a moment, then said:

"We are on Earth all right. Corda has just confirmed it for me. But it is ancient Earth. Or at least ancient to us. Our date is, as you know, 3457. We are on Earth in 1670, or thereabouts."

"Can they get us back? I don't want to be on Earth in 1670. It's of no use to me, really." As Zoe rather angrily said that, an oldish farmer appeared from the brow of a sunlit meadow, and headed towards them. Zoe and the captain turned to monitor his work-hard approach. He was before them in moments. He didn't materialize; he simply walked. They could smell him instantly. He smelt of bad bodily odours interlaced with dead animals, stale blood, and the dank aroma of soil. Zoe almost gagged.

"Bon nu-" he half croaked, then said something else. Then he suddenly seemed taken aback. It suddenly appeared as though the man, on second glance, didn't recognize who, not to mention what, these people were. At first he gave the impression that he might have known them; but not now. Now he *did not* know them! Now, he backed away in the quiet sunshine, wary, as they altered shape.

"It - is - all right," Peeler Curvature said in slow pronunciation. "We mean you no harm." He held up a grey hand as though confirming this statement. The man had by now observed his square feet, too, as well as his unusual attire, and his strange, slightly big flat face. Because of all this, he decided to turn to run. However, instead of running, he tripped over himself, and Zoe went to help him.

""We are from another country," she reassured him. "We are not from here." She spread her arms around as she spoke in a slow, augmented gesticulation. Then, seeing he couldn't understand, she helped the man to his feet. To her chagrin the man had solid shit dried on his rags of trousers - as though, shitting himself, he hadn't even removed them - let alone wiped himself afterwards. He was dirtier than Zoe could ever have imagined anyone from the past being. It exasperated her, curiously. "No," she then said angrily, "we are from a great spaceship!" She pointed up at the sky.

"He is pure baryonic matter!" Peeler Curvature calmly commented. "Could we imagine him aboard Favola? Hmmm. Interesting." He watched as Zoe helped the man up, as though observing an experiment. He made no attempt to help.

The Reason: Favola had known that neutrons and protons had been lost in the universe at some stage in the universe's history. But, after just five-hundred years of travelling outwards from Earth, it had eventually found them, and had noted upon it. Vastly hot rivers of invisible gas, which encircle all galaxies, concealed them. That's where the neutrons and protons had gone, which Earth's scientists even in the 25th century had completely lost track of. They were invisible within the invisible gas, which was itself hotter than a holographic star. They still existed, but in another level of reality. Consequently, everything that conscious creatures could see and feel, all the tangible *baryonic matter* in level-1 of the universe, that was created at each bang-ripple, but would eventually turn invisible inside super-hot gases, would begin the process of the *crunch-ripple* (or Big Crunch) by this transformation. Neutrons and protons mutated into a type of conscious transmutation.

This, now, for Peeler Curvature, somehow made itself crystal clear. It was as though, in watching Zoe help the dirty man to his quaking feet in an experimental remoteness, a theory had been confirmed. Was this, he reasoned, because he'd been placed on Earth in the 1600s? How could it be? What would that have to do with baryonic matter anyway? he asked himself. Every 10-billion years or so in the life of each universe Peeler Curvature knew that about half of baryonic matter eventually went missing - or at least it did to the myriad advanced-life scientists on hundreds of planets throughout every cosmos observing it. But now, in the presence of a farmer from

France's 17th century on Earth in *this* cosmos, Peeler Curvature knew for sure that once baryonic matter began to go missing then that was the exact point of no-return for every universe. From then on in the Big Crunch, heralding, ultimately, a brand new holographic universe, all altered, and was under way. It would be the end of any growth, anywhere within a current universe. And dark-matter's more mysterious dark-energy was a substance which made up 95% of this universe, as was known, but was responsible for retaining every single leaf, blade of grass, hair, eye, and drop of water, forever - beyond every universe – beyond any demise.

Dark-matter's haloes ringed every galaxy. It shaped not only the Earth, but ultimately everything that had ever existed in the Metaverse hologram. *Dark-matter was God, really!*

"I have seen the tangible past," Zoe Halloway then whispered somewhat sagaciously to the bedraggled man's face, as though telling him this fact. The man naturally did not understand; Zoe again felt a wonderment at the man's stench, as well as what she seemed to be experiencing via the location. "Is this," she went on, "the past? Am I in… the past?" She looked at it.

The man gazed at her now with abject horror. He spoke something terrifying in old French, as Zoe and the captain transformed. They did not look to him as they did to each other. They were from another time-fabric and different layer of the hologram. (3, probably). Consequently, the man's earthly eyes saw only their other-worldliness - their sheer alien transcendentalism. To him they not only looked like blobs, but vibrating, talking, moving blobs! Yet Zoe and Peeler saw the man as he was. They saw him as a man - an earthling from the long-ago past. Again he attempted movement.

Then, watching him, both Peeler and Zoe began to feel decidedly unwell. So much so that they had to sit down in the dry grass almost instantly. They looked at each other, both sensing that each practically felt the same. So, Peeler Curvature unfurled a different implement to monitor himself. The man looked at them from a distance, grasping his head. He stood stone still. Suddenly, they appeared to him as people again. Now, he was confused as well as frightened - as perhaps only the simplest can be - that is, he was moaning and shaking in hairbrained fear. Magnificently, there was a swift crack in the sky above them. Instantly a fabulous Alternative Craft - number 2 - appeared in the air directly over their heads in a deep humming sound. It appeared like a vision. Corda was piloting it, alone…

The man, seeing this, fell flat to the ground and covered his ears in the wind-rush. The craft landed just paces away from Peeler and Zoe, and a door opened. There stood Corda, as big and heroic as anything imaginable, hands on hips. He/she stepped from the craft and dashed at atomic speed to the two stricken comrades. Lifting first the captain, then Zoe with the other powerful arm, then nodding to the man on the ground as if acknowledging that he would be all right, Corda leapt back to the craft and into it very swiftly carrying them both, acting gently, but, as Zoe half saw it, with tremendous power.

On placing the captain down in a seat: "Sir, it suddenly seemed imperative that I acted personally to retrieve you and our guest. There was nothing else for it but the Alternative Craft. The time-fabric which you had both gone into was becoming highly unstable. You would have both been stranded on Earth in 1670. Not ideal, I venture to say. I covered the distance via a local wormhole. There is one already forming as we speak, close to one of Earth's neighbouring planets - Neptune, I believe it is called. We can, on your command captain, return to it in moments." Corda then stood erect and got positioned at the standing controls.

"Thank you, Corda," sighed the captain. "You did the right thing. You can get us out of here now…" Peeler Curvature looked to Zoe, who gazed up at Corda, now at the controls, now totally calm as before, not in the least flustered.

"You saved our lives," she sighed, now awed at this tiny spacecraft which also had technology beyond her understanding. "You acted independently to save us! I am deeply grateful, Corda."

"Think nothing of it. It is my duty."

"No, Corda," said the captain. "You did more than your duty. I cannot imagine what Zoe and myself would have done to survive on Earth in its deep history. What would have become of us?" He held his head momentarily at this thought, as he began recovering from his strange and unpleasant nausea. He briefly glanced out of a porthole to the man on the ground whom they'd left behind, and who, from that moment on, would relate his fantastic tale to all who gave him ears. They were off - in a second.

CHAPTER FOURTEEN

THEY MOVED SWIFTLY THROUGH level-1 of the holographic universe.

As Corda piloted the Alternative Craft into the spiralling void of the wormhole, and Zoe Halloway momentarily watched with amazement Neptune's size and shades glimmering before her, Peeler Curvature began focusing on, as he saw it, the tasks to hand. Yes, Earth really *was* an oasis - compared to many other planets he'd visited - but he was perplexed to comprehend that it was a real experience. Was he actually there? Had he actually gone back in time within the hologram, *to Earth?* This could happen in level-2, he knew, where consciousness became tangible again within an astral-field, and any level of reality could be accessed thereon. Yet, his instruments had told him that he'd not been placed in level-2, or 3, or even 4. (They did not go to 5, or beyond. Beyond level-5 in the holographic universe nothing could be monitored by anything on board Favola). No. He had remained in level-1, and not in hyperspace, either. He'd remained in so called *real time,* within the first level of reality in the universe. But time-shifts, he knew, always altered something. Something was always misplaced (or shifted) with time-shifts. That was how the universe worked, and this was what now concerned Peeler Curvature the most: *what would be shifted* from his and Zoe's materialization in Earth's past? Were they, actually, in *superposition,* as Favola had been? That is, in *two* places at the same time? It is possible, he knew. Superposition could be accessed from level-2 upwards. But could it be achieved inside level-1?

And the other information concerning the alloy?

Yes. The rare alloy on the planet *was* the other information on his mind. It was actually dark-matter made tangible. That's what the information was, via Favola. That's what the rare alloy was: dark-matter made real! The implications of this could be tremendous, he thought. Dark-matter had been discovered which had become an actual alloy! A dark-alloy, even. Peeler Curvature could hardly believe his own infused brain-waves. It was incredible, not to mention *incomprehensible.* Dark-matter was the alloy they'd been searching for, on the planet! Finally! An invisible weighty nothing, into a visible dense something? The implications would be fantastic.

"We are now entering the wormhole," Corda quietly advised his passengers. "Please brace for any movement." There wasn't much, but, upside down, it was intriguing to watch Corda handle the vibration at the controls while standing without a flicker. Zoe watched him, watching too Neptune vanish into a blackness, (the Neptune of Earth's 17th century) that instantly transmogrified into white, then to grey, then to a sort of pale green. It was a definite tunnel they were in. For certain. Zoe could even make it out as such: they were spiralling through a tunnel!

"So this is a wormhole..." she gulped, holding firm a handle, and, before even blinking, suddenly arrived on the vast rim of Favola. Its orbital lopsideness appeared as big as a planet itself in the dark, silent blackness of outer-space. Curiously, she then found herself not wanting to return to Earth, ever. Never. "This is so great," she whispered, turning to view the small wormhole close instantly behind them out of a porthole in the Alternative Craft. "It's like everything I could ever dream of coming true! It's so wonderful. I... never want to leave it!"

Corda, hearing her whispers, (Corda could actually hear grass grow, and had even recorded the sound of it in an experiment some six-hundred years ago) then told her that, "It would be biologically impossible for you and your children to survive for a long period aboard Favola, madam. Your biology needs sunshine and fresh air to keep it sustained. The things of Favola the inhabitants were grown accustomed to across myriad generations. I'm afraid, even though we sense your longing, that you simply must return to Earth for your own health. Indeed, that is probably one of the reasons why our guests briefly sent you there: you appear quite regenerated!" Corda spoke as he/she piloted the small craft across Favola's flattened bulk, towards an opening docking-bay hidden on the glinting surface.

"I do feel marvellous," Zoe then said, not really listening to Corda. "Captain, I have never felt this good in my life! Would it at all be possible for me and my children to stay on Favola, forever? I mean, could we be altered in some way to live here for centuries, just like you?" She gazed at Curvature on the seat next to her in a kind of hankering thirst for his approval.

… Who slowly shook his head. "We cannot alter life in the universe. It is one of our aphorisms. You have already had the most unique experience in the history of mankind to date! That in itself is surely reward enough? What about your husband, your career? What about your life on that lovely planet we've just been to? No one has stepped into the past as far as I know, only to return to their own time again. No, Zoe, we will return you to Earth at your time as soon as possible. I agree with Corda. It is imperative." He then stood to watch Corda slowly take the craft across the glimmering exterior of his greater craft below, in an air of heated disappointment, seemingly – but at what?

"I understand," said Zoe, watching him stand and reading him. "But I could be of use to Favola. My children could grow up as unique inhabitants, too. I, I, truly love it here with all this… unbelievable technology!" She gazed around, touching things. "It's so… spectacular to an earthling!" she then mused. "I have walked on

Earth, in Earth's past. Huh. Difficult to comprehend…"

Peeler Curvature gazed back at her as though concerned, perhaps, for her sanity. She had, after all, been through a lot, he thought. He watched her giggling, and his thoughts were instantly relayed to the 10-dimensional beings, who had already placed the future into creation for them, as well as that trip into the past - also intervening in Earth's overall past, often. The Aztecs, for example, had met them, and had briefly learned how to design spectacular cities from alien planets. Tenochtitlan, was an alien word. It meant, as close as they knew, *solid.* The Aztecs also knew and used gold, which came directly from the supernova that exploded to create Earth's solar-system. Gold was abundant for the Aztecs. Gold was pure. Gold was also very old, older than the Earth, as has been said. And if you removed the 'L' from the word gold, then what did you get?

God(s) moved in mysterious ways, was an Earth-placed saying. But it was true. They did. The 10-dimensional godlike creatures moved in very mysterious ways, and witnessed that particular supernova at close-hand, (mysteriously) and monitored its every flowing wave. It was supernovas that had them intrigued, ultimately. For in supernovas that had escaped their harness it was known that new particles were formed which would ultimately be key to them transgressing the Big Crunch - which they already felt they could accomplish. Then, the next new universe to be formed would be completely controlled by whichever advanced species came through, in its entirety!

Zapp. Back on the bridge, engulfed in Favola's own quiet music again, with Zoe's two children spirited there by the creators in her absence, Corda relieved the officer whom he/she had placed in charge of Favola, and attempted again to regain the ship. This time there wasn't a problem. The 10-dimensional creatures had already relinquished it. In fact there was no trace of them aboard in the interim. It was, Corda was then astonished to firmly discover via Favola, their minds which were there, and which were their technology on their hyper-planet. That is, their minds had advanced beyond any conceivable notion of software or hardware - at any point in the distant future for any civilization other than a Type III. Everything was monitored, acted upon, engineered, removed, by their minds - usually together as one whole gigantic energy-force. Tranced, as Corda received this information from Favola, which had itself begun regulating sections cerebrally, he/she felt, as far as he/she could tell, different. Corda was feeling mysterious…

"Xenon, we have just had a remarkable experience!" Zoe then told the overseer Xenon Ream as though she'd known him for years. She was standing, holding her head, smiling at her children, clearly ecstatic. "We've just been to

Earth! We just walked in the past, on a French meadow!"

"Yes, er, I know," the overseer calmly responded. "Corda eventually tracked you, you see. What was it like? Was it the same as the Earth you know?" He didn't really know what to say: Earth was Earth, to him, from what he'd read. The period seemed irrelevant.

"Oh, no! It was entirely different. Nothing like the Earth I know! There was a great silence, and a strong blue light, and lovely smells everywhere. There were distant hills that seemed to glow and go on forever! I'd like to go back. For a holiday. Would that be possible, captain?" She was serious.

"You know the answer, Zoe," Peeler Curvature humourlessly commented, standing next to Corda at the helm. "We did not engender that trip. We cannot do things like that. And besides, that man did not smell too good!" This was mirth coming through – though not terribly successfully.

"Man?" asked Xenon Ream, now interested. "You met a human being? A human being saw you both? He… he… must have been transfixed, terrified!" He raised a long arm.

"Only when Corda landed the Alternative Craft almost next to him!" croaked Zoe. "It was so amazing to see that vehicle come out of the blue sky like that. Totally wonderful. The man fell to the ground then. He's probably still running as we speak!"

"He's running into the past," Peeler Curvature

cryptically interposed.

"What I find incomprehensible," Xenon Ream then ruminated, "is the idea that, the man you saw, alive and well, is actually going on with his life now, even though it was thousands of years ago! He lives - somewhere. It is so strange, this universe of ours. Time is a curious concept. Once given light, always, it seems, to live! But, of course, being there like that did not give you the notion of being there like him: you went there with your minds, from your time. You would have needed to've been born and brought up in that time, and in that culture, to know what living at that time felt like. But then, ah, you wouldn't have known anything else! Also the actual language. You speak our tongue Zoe as you're from our era. But if you returned to Earth now, 3457, then I conjecture that you couldn't communicate, even in English!"

"Sir," Corda then cut in, "Favola informs me that we have a message from our departed guests. It seems they have been preparing to make the jump from the Big Crunch to the next Big Bang since Earth's 22nd Century. They believe they can, if we so desire, bring Favola along with them too! If true, this is remarkable information, sir. It seems we have new friends, although I cannot locate them anywhere on the ship. They must have - or presumably – departed!"

Peeler Curvature paused before speaking. "Are they saying that the crunch-ripple is imminent? I have a strong intuitive feeling that our friends actually dwell within the realm of dark-matter on a hyper-planet, where they've probably returned to. Hence how they're always close at hand. I cannot prove this, but I somehow know it. If so, then the dark-matter which we already monitor, and which encircles every galaxy we've traversed as a visible halo, must be where they dwell. This would explain their inter-dimensional transportation, as well as their extensive capacity for universe-outside thought. Corda, instruct Favola that I wish to meet with them once more!"

"I shall *try,* sir. But you know how they play with us."

"Captain," Zoe Halloway then declared while holding her two children in a similar standing position as when she first arrived, "I would like *very* much to survive this crunch-ripple you talk about! Can you imagine? A brand new universe at our finger-tips! Surely you couldn't turn that one down? Oh, captain, we could all be there together, forever!" She kissed both Clarest and Zen on their heads independently. "I want to be there with them, captain!" she softly added.

At that moment Ply Prism entered the bridge and Zoe and her children literally vanished as in a de-materialization, only to reappear at Vicinity 20 again. In her shocking absence, the captain and Xenon Ream stepped back to look at the spot from where she'd disappeared, in great discomposure. As though in a cloud of dust. Ply Prism seemed to know what had transpired…

"Sir," Corda then gasped, "our guests' are back! They are at present in Vicinity 20, along with Zoe Halloway and her children. Shall I take action, captain?"

"They're keeping me from her!" Ply Prism then hysterically suggested. "They sense I'm getting too close! They're keeping us apart! Captain, I now know since my sojourn with them that it is their overall project to survive the transition of the collapse of the seven layers of this universe. I feel that without Favola, however, in some way, they cannot achieve this!" He looked *to* the captain.

… Who said, "Take no action as yet, Corda," concerned also at Ply Prism's discomposure. "My present priority is to get down to that planet and test this rare alloy. If it truly is dark-matter made real, then we have, ah, found our gold. A great discovery!"

Ply Prism's feelings were all over his grey face: that Favola was initially brought into being by the creators in order to sustain some kind of ultimate void as the universe collapses, which they could then escape through. What, he'd further been wondering, would eventually become of the craft, as the millennia pressed towards that rendezvous? He had a lot on his mind. "They made us for a reason, captain - even if it is a selfish reason," he felt the need to say. "We are a major part of their survival plan! I now know this for sure. We may even evolve into something that might actually *look* like a survival plan!." His unusual thoughts made his face twitch.

"It could be that what you're suggesting is - and this is my angle on it - Favola would be a retaining memory-bank for them into the next universe?" the captain said quickly. "Does that seem plausible, Corda?" he then asked, pressed seemingly *for* that distant notion: time, and pressed also to take involuntary action, "do we have enough time for us to make our tests before the lines-of-force are aligned to return Zoe and her children to Earth? Give me the nano-seconds."

"I truly cannot say, captain. Now that they are back, and in Vicinity 20, I suspect we are at their mercy once more. I can give you the nano-seconds, yes."

"No matter," the captain said. "We go down anyway! Xenon, will you accompany my chosen team? Your knowledge of alloys is second to none. Ply, you will go too. Corda and myself will remain on the bridge, monitoring your every move…"

"There is a member of the astronomer-species I would like with me," Xenon Ream then submitted. She is an alloy specialist also. Her name is Alsing Furiant."

"She may not wish to leave their vicinity," said Ply Prism. "You know how they are."

"If Xenon wants her," said the cpatain, "then I will order it. Yes. We go to the alloy!"

Watching Peeler Curvature, the overseer felt a pang of concern for his sanity. He didn't seem to be acting quite as he should, Xenon Ream surmised. He seemed inorganic suddenly. Or just manic. It was difficult to say. There was something odd about him, though, and it appeared to be, to the overseer, his mental health. Xenon Ream was not sure whether or not to override the captain's orders.

Meanwhile, Zoc Halloway and her children (speaking of mental health) were once again engulfed in her enlarged moment-by-moment life on Earth. Used by the 10-dimensional creatures in a way that could never be made known *or* even clear to anyone but themselves, as it was interrelated to energy, and white energy's effect on dark's, Zoe now hovered at a low height amongst all her perfect, augmented memories. While it was true that the human memory, relying when in flesh only on a flabby, short-lived brain, faded fairly rapidly, it was but a trace of the experiences which it could relay to the mind holographically. That's all that could be recalled at a later date by the human brain: a trace. Everything else, however, every second of it, was the mind's way of storage in a holographic library.

What was recalled was recalled in the present, too, and therefore seemed regretful. (The present was a difficult concept to behold, of course, as it was seemingly fleeting). All the personal human experiences became just traces in the brain of what they once meant: for the actual 'experiences' were missing, it seemed. But, thanks to Vicinity 20's astonishing power, size, and supernatural accuracy

- along with the alien's force and subatomic manipulations - the experiences of one's life became ultra-graphically connected up again, and were, for all intent and purposes, lived more fully. The extra-experiences were no longer missing, seemingly. Recall meant something entirely different in Vicinity 20, as Zoe Halloway had discovered. If it happened 30 years ago, it became a huge reality. If it happened 30-minutes ago, there it still was. It was actually inside the skin, acting on the nerves, connecting up the brain to the emotions of the lived initial experience - whose lack was the apparent regretful part of the human memory…

CHAPTER FIFTEEN

EVENTUALLY THE LINES-OF-FORCE were perfectly aligned on the bridge by Corda and the captain using the alien's calculations - which entailed taking the moment-in-time from the recent black hole fly-through and use its ancient collapse-location coordination in the universe to achieve the alignment via 28-dimensional calculations - while the team landed on the green and purple planet with the rare dark-matter alloy. Zoe Halloway, though, was by then completely immersed in her minute-by-minute life on the big screen once more, in the hallowed hall of Vicinity 20…

No, she had become 'it' even more than her actual life on Earth!

Mars, Venus, Mercury, *and* Earth. The inner planets to Zoe's solar-system. Only the outer planets, she now knew - Jupiter, Saturn, Uranus, Neptune, Pluto, along with all the moons - had the potential for uninterrupted alien visitation, as they also had the potential for wormhole-formation via their spacetime bendy weight. And they *had* been visited - continuously. They'd been visited and explored by over a thousand different sentient species since the days of Earth's dinosaurs. Over a thousand of them. Even Type III civilizations had walked on these planets - or at least floated. Yes, Earth's solar-system was well known in the cosmos: Type IIIs had even been *to* Earth - often in the guise of domestic animals so as not to cause a stir, albeit playfully…

Floating, Zoe Halloway now knew that the true nectar of the gods was, crazily enough, chocolate. In fact that was one of the reasons why civilizations had visited other planets: they sought different tones and tastes of pleasure. It sounded insane, but it had been that way for millions of years.

Chocolate! Zoe could smell the stuff now. Earthlings only latched onto it fairly recently - in universe-age time. For chocolate was an alien recipe given to both the Aztecs and the Incas, possibly simultaneously - and was still very much prevalent in Zoe's time on Earth. It would then be left to develop within that community, only to be sampled at a later date by whichever species made a return.

CHOCOLATE! Aliens, in the guises of domestic dogs, say, have lapped at it for millennia!

And the sweet word resounded in Vicinity 20, along with its myriad tastes. *PLEASURE,* it said to Zoe. For that's what it equalled, and that's what most advanced alien civilizations searched for. *PLEASURE* - in whichever form. They'd searched, they'd found, they'd conquered, (they'd certainly indulged, *and* played) - and not just with chocolate. For the alien taste-bud was quite phenomenal. The lucky earthlings (and there were some who witnessed them as they really were) who happened to be there at the time, also indulged with them, often literally. They just went along for the ride: the list is long, starting with Caligula. But that was just how early earthlings indulged - at the base level. Aliens took pleasure in many advanced things - as well as watching earthlings indulging, which had amused them no end. Now, Zoe Halloway's name could be added to that human pleasure-witnessing list, as she had tasted as *they* had tasted. Or, perhaps her son could. Zen Halloway, although a boy, would be visited as a young man at a later date by the 10-dimensional creatures on Earth - and not just as either dogs or cats, as was their wont. He'd go along with them for the ride, as it were, and would be indulged in in the most heightened forms of pleasure, which, it could be argued, were the pleasures of the mind interlaced with the flesh, though not sexually. (The pleasures from a so called 'cultured' mind could be quite exalted, as was known. But coupled with the tangible senses?)

The captain was, to his astonishment, allowed then into Vicinity 20 to meet with the 10-dimensional creatures, whose appearance to the inhabitants had been becoming clearer since Zoe Halloway's sojourn into Earth's amazing past. Hazy at first, they were now quite distinct to a 3-dimensional eye.

Since the alignment, he'd been on his way there by float-car - not really expecting to be allowed in, nor to see them. He was aghast to find the huge doors opening for him on his arrival, as if remotely for a special guest. He eased himself from the float-car and stood alone in the silence of light wind and perennial polyphonic music. (To him this *was* silence). He took one step towards Vicinity 20, and suddenly the four 10-dimensional creatures were there before him - writhing, as indeed Zoe had suggested, in white. Or was it pale green?

Shocked at what he saw, Peeler Curvature was immediately put at ease right down at the base of his now vibrating mind. He was then *encased* in ease. No, in happiness. Intense, multi-dimensional happiness. He felt an immediate happiness that none of the pleasure-domes or anything else he knew could bring. It was, he saw, an overwhelming extra-dimensional happiness. The sort that made you want to close your eyes in the knowledge that you are going to exist for all time. And that's what he did: he smiled inwardly, warmly, to which the advanced beings acknowledged with a simultaneously tilt of their (what looked like) heads - equally as warmly.

"… We, too," they cryptically whispered in the same 24th Century pickled English. "We are happy to be in your presence, captain. You have remarkable powers - for a human-species! However, are you fully prepared for Favola's dip into the planet's final moment? You may not be. You did well getting the calculations correct, but you haven't accounted for what will happen when you actually put them into practice, as you're about to do. Just moments to go, captain."

"The alignment is set," the captain said, "but the implosion is still minutes away. We are motionless in space before it, awaiting our instant light-thrust. The motion-drives are, indeed, primed. However, I have a feeling that once it takes place we may not witness you again. Is this true?" Peeler Curvature gazed at the creature's almost beautiful outlines and seeming texture, which was that of goldleaf, he felt, even though he didn't touch it, waiting for an answer. Indeed, in some respects, they were animated-liquid green-white metal, only not metal. And not liquid. And not really any colour, either. Just free-moving form, seemingly, in lights. A living illumination, in fact. Here, there, then closer, then further away, all lit up. And wistful. Wistfully close. But beautifully distant at the same time - alienly illuminated heavenly, was a phrase. Peeler Curvature didn't really have the words. The aliens are beautiful, he thought, and that did it for him. He was almost stunned before them because of it.

"Something you haven't planned will transpire when you dive at the planet," the creatures said in simple terms. "It will not be harmful, but it is necessary that it takes place. Have no fear."

"What will happen? What in Favola are you telling me?"

"The moment-in-time from the black hole will engender it. No harm will come to you, captain. We can assure you of that. But it is vital that what transpires, transpires. That is how the universe dictates things at the level of calculation you have now undertaken…"

And as the captain further tried to get out of them what would happen without his prior knowledge, the handful of human-species had departed the Alternative Craft on the planet, and were walking the short distance to the dark-matter alloy, under a purple haze, in golden life-support suits.

The planet had an atmosphere, which gave a deep purple shade to everything under its gleaming sun - whose other twin star was, as has been said, neutron. But that also could be seen; and the curious pulsing light *it* gave flickered through the purple haze in a ghostly aura of jagged silhouettes. Gazing up at these silhouettes as she walked, the astronomer-species known as Alsing Furiant, who did indeed have to be ordered from the sequestered Vicinity 91, watched with her one larger eye dust from the dry environment get blown upwards to mingle in this astonishing sky, creating even more silhouettes. She was very interested to watch it: it was a very interesting phenomenon to behold. Ply Prism led the team; Xenon Ream as overseer followed last of all. Curiously, there weren't any rocks or boulders or meteorite craters to be seen on the landscape - just dust and an intensely purple sky…

Then the alloy was suddenly located.

Warped, seemingly - although it had no

recognizable shape - its height and width was remarkably large. And swollen, too. Yet it was not observed on the horizon, or even from many paces away. Then it just disappeared. No. It didn't disappear, it appeared in another shape. But then it did disappear. It was vanishing, transforming metal. Nothing could be more alien to any species anywhere: vanishing metal with a seeming will of its own? A see-through solidity?

Ply Prism was transfixed in his comfortable life-support suit, his eyes as wide as old-fashioned pies on Earth. The diamond-probe was there with them, hovering alongside the four of them - the fourth member being a female officer-species who only spoke to give commands. It was relaying things back to the 10-dimensional creatures – detailed information that was beyond the understanding of even a Type II civilization. The diamond-probe had properties that only Type IIIs could ever comprehend.

The captain was now with Zoe Halloway, amidst her big-screen life. While no one had ever been violent on Favola, Peeler Curvature came close to the emotion of it, as he now fully comprehended that the aliens were running things aboard. Nothing was likely to physically happen to them, (nothing actually could) though an appeasement might have been preferable. Or so the captain somewhat childishly mused. Then, as Favola counted down for the light-speed dive at the doomed planet with Corda in control, and, doing two tasks at once (leaving the team alone on the other planet's surface with a slick Aternative Craft that had life-support for many Favolan days) the captain suddenly felt the need to get physical. He felt the need to actually take carnal action, which even astonished him!

The instant acceleration, however, while normally having no effect, *had* an effect, and, as two large suns were close by, and Peeler Curvature fell at Zoe Halloway, who yelped and fell at her kids, who in turn screamed and were saved by the aliens - *flash!* - the planet imploded like a dying sun, almost creating a black hole in the spectacular process! But it wasn't large enough to do that. Instead, as Favola intermingled with its nano-second de-atomization, then shot beyond the location at precise light-speed, the hyperspace also was triply inflated - so the captain became transformed. He changed into a floating, slow-motion sort of gloworm. He gagged on his own constricted throat.

In an instant Favola was slowly orbiting the Earth once more. Coming out of hyperspace before even entering it, before even registering that it had gone into it, Favola had shaken up spacetime drastically…

The usual magnificent blueness to the planet Earth that all previous human beings knew and loved appeared altered - kind of dulled. It was a darkened kind of blue, and Corda was suddenly monitoring it on the bridge. A different blue. Also, there was a lot of space-traffic: it was literally lined up, bumper to nose, encircling the great globe beneath it - all shapes and sizes. There were thousands of small space-vehicles attached to various trajectories, just travelling around the earth to their various destinations. But to where? Transdoors were used in Zoe's time, and would no doubt be used for a long time *after* Zoe's time - or an advanced form of it. So why so many spaceships?

On free-floating in Vicinity 20, to a falling standstill, Peeler Curvature orientated himself and dusted himself down as himself once again before speaking to Corda on the bridge. "Corda, what goes on? Zoe and her children are still with me. Was the blast successful? Where are we?" He looked to Zoe, who fell to her knees in a vacuous state. Her life had been removed from the cone-screens and her children seemed cold and desolate in the great arena. Peeler Curvature scanned around for the 10-dimensional creatures. They were seemingly very absent.

"Sir, you need to return to the bridge. We are orbiting Earth: but the time is, er, *our* time. It is Earth in 3457, I believe. This time, however, we have indeed already been tracked!" The captain held his ear-implant as he received this information. But then, without either his or Corda's authorization, to say nothing of action, Favola began moving slowly *towards* the Earth - as though on an entry-trajectory into the very atmosphere. "Sir," Corda then cut in, "we are now entering an orbital trajectory which will take us into Earth's atmosphere. Our velocity has slowed down to an astonishingly slow rate: I fear we will either burn up or actually be too big for the atmosphere to hold us! Our energy-outputs cannot sustain the craft airborne in a 1-G environment!"

"Take no action, Corda! Our friends warned me of this. I trust them when they tell me that no harm will come to us. I'll be with you presently." The captain then attended to Zoe and her children, as he also glanced up at the cone-screens: Earth loomed large on them in great graphic detail.

'I'm afraid I must act, sir. It is in my nature. I am attempting to regain control. But it seems our trajectory has already been ordained by our amalgamation with the de-atomized planet at light-speed, Favola informs me. What transpires now is all part of our computation to acquire amalgamation. There is nothing we can do about it, captain: we are entering Earth's atmosphere!"

"… We are not doomed, Corda. I know this."

"Perhaps we are, sir. Favola now informs me that our current slowing speed is indeed allowing us to gently descend into the atmosphere, without any friction, but we are too big to be controlled in an atmosphere, as you know. Our gravity may also effect the weather-systems. Our size is too enormous for any atmosphere!" Then, as Corda went to begin another sentence, Peeler Curvature himself, Zoe and her two children, materialized on the bridge from out of a bright, colourful halo.

Greatly shaken, Zoe Halloway then froze as she stepped from the halo and watched - while orientating herself from 'watching' in Vicinity 20 - Earth's enormous features loom graphically up across the great viewing-screen. Slowly they got bigger, as Favola descended into the planet and Corda fought against it. She took a nervous step back, and held her mouth.

"Sir, according to my readings," Corda said loudly, struggling slightly, "you are and should still be at Vicinity 20! This is quite remarkable. Observe." Corda watched Peeler Curvature as though amazed, then pointed at his living readings on an instrument, showing him still in Vicinity 20. Yes, it was superposition. The hows and whys could wait.

For the captain had more pressing concerns. "Well, I seem to be here now," he glibly remarked. "Here *and* there! There is nothing we can do to alter our present course of descent. We are in their hands. Corda, the team? Are we still able to contact them? Are they still on the planet at the far side of the galaxy - alone?"

"Yes, sir. As far as I can tell. All their readings are normal. But then, as we've just seen with *your* readings, nothing seems certain any more. Hard as I try, we are going in towards the Earth!"

Within moments Favola had broken through Earth's upper atmosphere, engendering great lightning flashes in the process. A landmass below could now be seen; though nothing could as yet be made out. Twenty or thirty flying crafts were soon up along side Favola's vast rims, dwarfed by comparison. Contact was soon being made, though it was a global English that had developed into something beyond Corda's understanding. It was the English of the 35th Century, with a myriad new words absorbed, a myriad new meanings…

"Sir, Favola informs me that a multi-communication is being attempted in what she deems to be advanced English - recognized by what appears to be the curious speculation of multi-generational offspring from distant adjectives and nouns. She is attempting to translate…"

"We are going in no matter what!" the captain then gasped. As he said that, the landmass which appeared below that was once known as Australia, which was surrounded by ocean, was now surrounded by an ocean in freeze. In fact, the entire globe was frozen in 3457, Favola then discovered, all down to Global Cooling through the removal of all C02 via enforced misinformation across centuries. Australia was no longer orange, it was white! The blue of the seas was grey!

"Sir, Favola tells me that we are required to identify ourselves. We are also being warned to back away, as our size is already hampering earth-bound communication. I fear they may take action, sir. Although, what they can do to us…" Corda monitored intensely the myriad craft circling the great ship, a ship whose lack of lights or any seeable distinctions made it appear most alien.

Then, things began to get very blurred for Zoe - fuzzy as in a dream. Alone, she now found herself on the ground, *on Earth,* under a great glass dome - like she had in fact known - but not glass, and not really a dome. She could see Favola directly above her, looking like some massive grey cloud half covering a grey-blue sky, hovering there. People, yes, human beings, were walking past her, looking at her as though watching something unusual. They were dressed in garments and fabrics which certainly she had never seen before, and were, it seemed, maddened. Perplexed, she now edged away on wobbly legs (how ancient she seemed) and attempted to communicate with a young woman. She stopped her through gesticulation, then said, "Hello. Is this Earth? I'm afraid I'm a little lost."

"Whado yup sam flup!" the young woman yelped, frowning as though angry. "Whado? Yup sam? Clast in how rid yup from leddth vron?" She shook her head.

"What?" yelled Zoe. "I, I, don't understand! Are you an earthling?"

"Thest cirew to gup!" The woman then yanked her blue-tinted arm from Zoe's hold and stormed away. Zoe was now, it seemed, a total alien on her own planet! At 35, she was a thousand-years old. She gazed up to look at the gigantic underneath of

Favola, awesome across this dome thing she was in, and felt distinctly lonely. In fact she felt a longing to be back aboard Favola, which itself suddenly seemed like an entire world within a world, a world in which everything and anything could happen in safety. It seemed like… home. This was not, clearly, the planet Earth that she had known and loved. What was this language in her thousand-year absence? (Not that she knew the date). Certain animals, too - ones which she had known, like dogs and cats - seemed to have evolved into, as far as she could tell, sentient beings. That is, they were walking around upright, (almost comically - perhaps a little sinister in their appearance) dressed in a similar manner to the people, and talking a similar tongue to the one in which the young woman spoke.

"Thest sam vron that shipatty?" a black man then asked, thumb-pointing up at Favola.

Zoe held her head and felt very panicky. For this was surely a vile but surreal dream! No. It was as real as anybody could know *real,* she told herself. Also, as people walked past buildings, the buildings, if such a word could still be used in 3457 to describe structures which people inhabited, altered. That is, they folded and flipped and flashed and divided, almost instantly. *They moved* - everything jumped. To an ancient, 25th Century person, it was ultra-bizarre!

Folding buildings? 'I'm sorry, I don't know what you said." Zoe stood perfectly still in this grotesquely spectacular world, and just watched it all either unfold or enfold itself around her - just as the universe did holographically. And then, while watching with her eyes wide open she saw above her head, beyond the dome, Favola leave its location and begin moving slowly, awesomely, away.

She saw too that everyone could *see* Favola; though no one took any notice of it in particular. To these future-speaking human beings the sight of a massive circular craft as big as a large island hovering at a low height, with lightning flashing all around it, did not merit more than a glance up! The technology here was so advanced from the old 25th century that nothing caught one's attention!

Or so it seemed to an isolated Zoe. Then she saw that people used Psychokinesis perfectly.

Mind over matter? Mind to move matter, to become matter? She saw them stop, close their eyes, then reappear in another location on the street, or up in a flipping, flopping, folding building! They'd achieved it. They could use their minds to travel! How utterly astonishing. These 'people' were no longer what Zoe Halloway could recognize as... *human.* They'd evolved further, gone beyond...

Earth, Favola would now discover, had become a Type II civilization.

CHAPTER SIXTEEN

THE GRAVITATIONAL PULL on Favola was enormous, much more than a black-hole in outer-space. As was its on the Earth. It seemed that this was what the earthlings were requesting of the great craft: that it should ease back into high orbit because of its gravitational pull, Favola translated. Not because they feared it or anything like that: it should ease back out into orbit for safety reasons. For it was so big that it was like a giant lid being pressed down on the planet, closing it. It was bigger than anything ever visited upon the Earth in a century. Too big, in fact, to actually see from close up, underneath: too big to be seen. It created night in the broad ice-age dome-day. It was like the moon bending down to kiss the Earth, one inhabitant would later write…

And then, Zoe saw Favola moving slowly away - lightning and all - in an atonishing sight, via a visual given her by the 10-dimensional creatures - who had actually visited Earth in 8457, never mind 3457! (They would never tell any human what Earth would be like then). Size, though, was why the people on the ground appeared maddened, though not awed. It was the 35th Century's equivalent of being angry. That this enormous spaceship was suddenly in their arena, messing things up, blocking things out? *Shipatty,* it would transpire, was the new global English word for spaceship. Though that word didn't cover something of this magnitude, and that also angered them. There was no new word for a flying world, even by 3457. There should have been, but there wasn't. Dome-night by dome-day, perhaps? And Zoe, still on the ground, was from that flying world, that shipatty. She was one of them!

More buildings flipped and folded without a sound as she ambled past under the induced darkness of Favola, then an old man appeared in front of her. He'd willed himself from up in a jumping building, to down into the glinting street - just like that. *Flip!* Hello. Only not hello - "Tica." Tica, was hello in 3457, Zoe Halloway would eventually discover. "Whado limpit sam to shipatty vron?" he croaked. (Old English translation: Do you need to get back to your ship?)

"I have no idea what you said," Zoe sighed, stopping to look at the man. He was old, really old. 300 or something. At least. He didn't actually *look* 300 - more like 90. His clothing, though, while clearly new and clean, was made from a material that Zoe had never encountered before, being from the distant past. (Imagine: Earth-time 1457. Someone from that era materializing in New York in 2457?) He wore glasses which could view all angles simultaneously, including up - a bit like the inhabitants viewing Zoe's face on Favola, minus the latter dimension. Confused? "I, I, think they're going to leave me here!" she then said, obviously upset, and sensing that she was talking to herself.

"My children are on that spaceship, you see. Look, it's going away! Oh, no. What am I going to do?" She gazed up at Favola's thick rims angling away from across the dome that she was in, moving upwards, slowly, awesomely, and began to actually sob.

"Oh," the old man then gasped, "a, a, person, ah, from, ah, the past! I can, ah, speak your ancient language - if, ah, I can get my head tuned in! Yes. That's better. Now then, my dear, what seems to be the problem? Oh, don't cry. Your friends won't leave you, I'm sure. That shipatty - our word for, ah, spaceship - will not go far. I've seen this before. Only-" The old man gazed up as though focusing on something, "not, ah, as big! Or at least not for a century, when people from Orion came. You must be from a very long time ago, judging by the way you speak!" He looked at her with some curiosity.

"You can speak - English! You can communicate - with me!"

"I can already speak English. I speak the English of my time, a language that has evolved from billions of people across a few thousand years. Standard English, your English, died out about 800 years ago now. However, it just so happens that I'm a specialist in that *ancient* English - ah, your English. I've studied it all my life. I'm a translator, you see. Are you familiar with the epic poem called *Gullah,* which dates from 2510-to-13? Almost 900 years ago! The greatest poem in the

English language, I'm told. I am one of just three people to have translated that poem into modern English! Now then, I'm assuming that you have leapt forward into the future somehow in your spaceship there." He glanced up again, as his strands of white hair blew around his craggy face. "Have no fear, no harm will come to you! We get visitations like this from time to time. They're usually safely delivered back to their own time. Huh, it really annoys the younger ones, though. They're so intolerant. Messes communications up, you see. Still, I suppose I was intolerant too when I was their age. Anyway, my dear, much as I'm enjoying our chat, I must be going. You'll be fine. It's just an anomaly." He blinked, and was gone. In an instant.

"No!" Zoe yelled. "Come back! I need your help! Please! There's a lot I want to ask you!" In *that* instant, Zoe herself vanished, only to materialize back on Favola's fabulous bridge...

Ply Prism was there, and he rushed to her aid. Clarest and Zen dashed to her limpness also.

What was happening was Favola's gravitational pull on the Earth was beginning to have an effect *on* the Earth, and the 28-dimensional calculations had taken this into account: a time-trajectory was now being introduced - almost like a great mechanism...

Favola then moved across the Earth in this time-trajectory, as though a vast creative force in itself. To the earthlings down below in their domes it was like watching an island uprooted and flying gently over the sky at low altitude. For it covered most *of* the sky, leaving only the edges to let in that dull blue. Two discs of black, with a symmetrical circle of light. It was like having land pressed against land, with just a slit of brightness on the wrap-around rim. Indeed, Favola seemed as big as the Earth - to those underneath it, gazing up at it, still annoyed.

Unbeknown to anybody, (except, oddly enough, Zoe's son, Zen) the 10-dimensional creatures were now right down at the quark-level during this flight. Spacetime was still in the process of being manipulated; for at the quark-level extra calculations could be carried out with more precision, ones which could not be done in a thicker dimension. And right down there, in the darkness of the deepest dark-matter, 7-dimensional conscious beings were now in communication with the 10-dimensional ones. Tiny, tiny, sub-sub-sub-creatures, with eternal consciousness. Astonishing entities. For as Favola traversed across the Earth, with Earth-time now aligned to Favolan-time, (Earth had, of course, as was said, evolved way beyond Favolan society, whose static existence would be eternally fastened at Zoe Halloway's epoch) the tiny 7-dimensional creatures worked for the 10-dimensional ones on request. The 10-dimensional ones were ultimately using Favola as some type of experiment towards the greater good of surviving the Big Crunch, as was also said, Zen would discover, who then said this:

"Mom, the white creatures are telling me that they are now very small. They're tiny. No one could see them with any instrument. They're doing things for us, mom. They're taking us home!"

"Your mother is traumatized," Ply Prism then said, holding Zoe as though he had feelings for her. "She cannot really hear what you're saying, Zen. It's okay, though. She'll be okay soon. I promise. Here. Sit, Zoe. You'll soon be leaving us and, and, I'll never see you again!" This notion suddenly hit Ply Prism as though, like the feelings themselves, he had never thought about it before. But now he was. He was thinking about it. He was thinking about the notion that - now an urge - any moment now Zoe would vanish and he would never see her again - either in this universe or the next! Never. Not once. Ever. It daunted him. No, it humbled him. Because, on Favola, human-species were around for an awfully long time, and, well, to put it bluntly, he didn't truly *feel* for any of them like, yes, he was *feeling* for Zoe.

He liked them, but he didn't feel for them. It was all new to him now, this feeling, this new liking! New, right at the end of it all. He hated the way the universe worked sometimes. Hated it. It was ghastly. It worked *against* you, it seemed. "Zoe, I…" He couldn't say it. Didn't have the adeptness. The gift was never there. Sex and love simply did not take place on Favola. No one had genitals. No one performed a reproductive act. There was no desire to. It was all done scientifically. All done with mirrors. Consequently, on this ultra-rare occasion when a human-species came into contact with, for all intent and purposes, an alien, and fell for this alien in a big way, the machinery wasn't there to back it up!

Favolans did not have the capacity for love. This may have been a tragic thing.

For my mother gazed into Ply Prism's eyes, and half smiled. Then, the great craft Favola actually touched down on the planet Earth - my planet. It landed! The very ground beneath it seemed to shake. For Favola's weight was possibly beyond estimation. But the old Earth took it - as it had taken lots of things in its long history. It took it. We landed in a remote northern part of North America, as I recall, not all that far away from where I came from - although a universe away in recognizability - and the Earth's outer-layers crumbled under our weight. The alien's diamond probe was by then my constant companion. It was my child's toy, always there at my side, watching me. As we landed, it came closer to me and touched my cheek with a sting of heat, doing something to me. The diamond probe then spoke to me of things that I couldn't understand, but of which nonetheless were absorbed. It spoke to me of otherness. The diamond probe was my go-between. It has since told me everything.

And it is still here today, right now, hovering

quietly - discreetly when needs be - and this is 40 years after that event! The diamond probe came with me, *is* me, looks out for me, speaks to me at all times. I also speak to it. It has my mind inside it. It is not an imaginary friend.

It turned out that my mother, Zoe Halloway, who, as you all know, became the first world-leader as Earth fully became a Type I civilization in the 2470s, was purposefully rescued from a probable fatal accident in the Transdoor just moments before it would have happened by the 10-dimensional creatures, known, incidently, as *Elevates,* thereby intervening on fate - which didn't actually exist anyway. Two things: (1) my mother couldn't die, as she had a destiny to fulfil: (2) she had to witness things way beyond her understanding and knowledge. For only then, at a deep, subliminal level, would she be equipped enough to become the very first world leader.

Zoe Halloway had a fantastic spiritually-advancing adventure!

She was to be abducted anyway - at a later date, I was told. The accident, which would have happened to my mother as she materialized from the Transdoor on the moon, would have been a mining accident, where things unsecured came loose at the exact wrong moment. She'd have been cracked over the head with something heavy, and killed. On the moon. But no. *My friends prevented it.* She materialized onto the bridge of Favola instead, and the rest you now know…

It seemed that by actually touching down on Earth in its own original spacetime, Favola then achieved our precise return, precisely. Don't ask me how - the universe moves in mysterious ways. And I mean literally. *It moves!* But it did. It got us back. It pulled out all the stops. Corda was also fantastic.

Comprehend this. Imagine every sun in a certain galaxy. It could be millions. It could be billions. Imagine the power of each of those suns together. A singular, roaring, cataclysmic, focused energy. Then imagine that isolated power directed to your fingertips, to control whatever phantasmagorical implement you have at your disposal. That's how the inhabitants of a Type III civilization exist. They have that power. They move through time as we moved through air. They are *beyond* the imagination of anyone outside of a Type II civilization, really. But I was allowed in. I have seen how they exist. I have been to their domain! The Elevates were pure in this sense: they were eternal. If a monotheistic god had ever existed, it seemed to me when I eventually studied religious history and the curious beliefs of humans, then it would probably choose *not* to exist - as to exist would be *impure.* Therefore, if God had ever existed, He would not exist out of choice! That's how it would have seemed to me had I been brought up in a time when people actually believed in such things. Thankfully I wasn't, so I didn't have to worry. But that's how I was thinking as a youngster. The Elevates, though, while having no infantile concept whatsoever of being pure, existed as God would have existed. That is, they created everything known to man, including man's creation of God, and man's creation of man, thinking *of* God!

And they let me in. I knew and still know who they were.

Back on Earth in 3457, it transpired that no one knew of the existence of Favola. There was no record of it that anyone could access. Everything had been lost (or erased) in a thousand years. So, Favola was alone, really. Not lost in space, but alone in the spacetime of the infinite universe, and it would just go on exploring until the Big Crunch, and then go on exploring after that, with the Elevates.

I alone retain the memory of Favola.

CHAPTER SEVENTEEN

THE MEMORY. MY MEMORY. *HUMANITY'S MEMORY...*

Yes, I alone retained the memory of Favola, all because I had that tiny stain of an infant brain-tumour removed with that Hymnus device. (All design, of course). This, it seemed, prevented the brain-washing which happened to my mother and sister (although my mother gained a spiritual-advancement from being on Favola) on our return. To me, Favola was all still very real, all still intense and weird and fantastic, even beautiful. To them, it never existed. Consequently, for decades afterwards my mother simply thought that I had imaginary friends, and that, well, I was a bit odd. (He's 30, and he's still talking about spaceships and 10-dimensional creatures!) Then she thought I was a medium; but nothing triggered her, and nothing ever would. The memory had completely gone from her and my sister. The Favolans, though, not only retained a memory of being back to Earth, but recorded everything in their Vicinity 20 and had downloaded the entire thing to every human-species' dream-sequences. They dreamt *Earth* for centuries, I was informed. The inhabitants of Favola actually had us in their heads: Earth became their dream-time home!

And Favola became my long-lost reality...

Antimatter. That was the word which was

privately in Xenon Ream's mind as the great craft listed in the black abyss. He had been afraid that Favola would act as antimatter upon the Earth and be vaporized in an instant. It didn't happen, of course. But he felt it could have. Favola was not antimatter - she was parallel-matter! Even so, Earth's pull was powerfully upon her for a period. Earth's gravity tugged at the parallel heart of Favola's inter-dimensional vastness - which was more wonderful, thanks to the Nebstron - than her human creators (from my time) could have ever imagined or planned. Indeed, Favola was and is the only concept of its kind in this universe, I now know. She was the great craft that listed in the forever black abyss! Yes, her creators certainly excelled.

Dark-matter, though, and dark-matter's dark energy, was the ultimate wonder of the universe. Dark-matter *is* the 'thing' in the universe, believe me. Dark-matter is darker than the darkest dark imaginable. It is so dark that it is actually light, though a light brighter than any starshine! And I have seen it. I have actually seen tangible dark-matter as light. It's where everything returns to after it has died, only to be re-made as new! Everything. It's where the universe's ultimate force is located.

Dark-matter *is* the Heaven and Hell which ancient humans spoke about!

But enough ranting philosophy. Peeler Curvature's team, naturally, harnessed the special dark-matter alloy from the purple planet, (where they saw a human face in the dust, astonishingly - though they put it down to a freak swirl of wind) and put it to use aboard Favola, darkly. They did this via the astronomer-species, led by Alsing Furiant, who, incidently, never got to meet my mother. (Had she met her, though, she would have told her, I know. She would have told her that the very 10-dimensional creatures whom she sort of got to know were in fact the Type III civilization from Earth's galaxy that would, when the time came for earthlings to finally make the vast jump to their Type III status, wipe them out. Blip. Gone. Sorry.) But, thankfully no. She never met her. Besides, Earth's giant step to a Type III civilization was a long way off. Yet it would happen - almost. We would almost get there. My friends, alas, the very creatures whom my mother actually met, would be the ones to eventually instigate Earth's instant demise, as was said. For there could only ever be one Type III civilization in any single galaxy, anywhere. That seemed to be a law of the universe. And, as there were billions of galaxies in the universe, there were billions of Type III civilizations. That, it could be argued, was enough.

Alsing Furiant worked ferociously on the lonely planet with Ply Prism to harness the exotic material. And 'harness' it needed - only not with straps: it was a lively alloy. Once aboard Favola (they only needed a small amount of it) the rare alloy then bounced and leapt as though alive. Bouncing, it would vanish. Reappearing, it would hang from ceilings. Flickering, it would glow-fade and almost moan. Down on the planet, though, things happened which human beings could never truly comprehend. Droplets of liquid, the size of footballs, fell very slowly and then sploshed on touch-down. As they sploshed, they gleamed glow-worm silver, then evaporated. More droplets would fall; a wind would then cause them to gently descend on weird tangents to the flat, purple-dusted ground. In the wind, the droplets made howling noises that might have frightened an earthling to death. For the droplets weren't water, they were an unknown liquid with the constituency of tree-sap. It wasn't nitrogen; it wasn't mecury. It was something new: it's components unknown to the inhabitants.

Yes, it was the most alien planet they'd ever encountered!

If it's revelations you're after, then now is the time, I feel. Now is the time for me to reveal to you just how our friends, the 10-dimensional creatures, actually subsisted. They were not *organic,* as we would know it. That much is probably clear. For they existed at super-cool temperatures, which enabled them to think at super-fast levels. No. They were, well, supernatural, in that they dwelled in the myriad dimensions of the dead, but also in our physical universe in an ethereal manner. Whereas our capacity for thought can only really function at room-temperature, so to speak - and fairly slowly at that - theirs transpired at a billion times faster, in their super-cold environment, and could actually make contact with flesh. Their thoughts touched you!

Because of this, this thought-touching, they could distribute concepts among different creatures simultaneously, while totally exhausting the creatures from the reception, as has been documented. Also, as the unconscious mind of every human being became the *conscious* mind at death, (phase-transition - a step into one's mind: the unconscious was the true conscious) and then existed as such in a type of energy-force within the vast and spectacular realms of dark-matter in holographic layers beyond number 1, the 10-dimensional creatures could communicate with them, as that also is where they dwell. Every dead creature ever, as that was what the holographic universe required, lived on. At varying levels, depending on their particular spiritual-advancement and conscious-understanding at the time of phase-transition, which then translated itself to the immortal unconscious/conscious mind, human beings and everything else, once born, never died. (It took the universe a long time to bring about conscious creatures like us. Do you think it just wipes us out after the eye-blink of life?)

The ones with a greater perception began eternity at a different holographic level to ones with, say, a more childlike perception - which would simply be nurtured *with* children for a century or so who had died before their time. No, not elitism as humans knew it. Just how it is. This is how it is in the universe when a living creature dies: no spiritual-advancement, equals a long time afterwards in the company of children - only they are the adults. Once we *do* advance, the 10-dimensional creatures are then able to impart with us on a much broader level. They are able to profoundly communicate. This opens me up to even more ridicule concerning the soul, etc. But you will eventually discover it for yourself when you finally phase-shift. Be patient: *we go on!*

Dark-matter is Nature, you see.

The planet Earth came about through dark-matter, and the Cosmos evolved consciousness on this planet (and others - only in a different way) in order that the consciousness should dwell after a fleshy start for the duration *of* the universe, but in another, truer, more-able-to-comprehend form. Or, a form that requires no maintenance at least. And, if our friends from our galaxy have anything to do with it, right through to the next universe, and so on, every leaf and spider, ad infinitum! That the Cosmos has allowed life is the very magic. That the life evolved awarness of itself is the magnificence. We are eternal children of the cosmos, and will, all of us, soar for eternity as conscious energy!

Take comfort.

Back on Earth in 2457 my mother awoke to find my sister and I asleep on the bed with her. It was a sunny day, and we had all been sleeping heavily, seemingly. Heavily, I awoke to simply recall Favola and Corda. Then I thought of the captain. There it all still was, in my mind. In fact, I thought we were still on board - until I recognized my mother's bedroom. I knew then that we had been sent back - but not, it appeared, to the exact moment before we were about to leave for the Moon in the Transdoor. No. For it was the morning of that day, not the moment before. Strange, I thought, waking as a child when one had adult thoughts in one's head. I sat up, and watched my mother stir back into life.

It was lovely to watch her face for a time, in the past, as it were, us all young and alive and so happy. It was lovely to see my mother again alive in flesh, as real as your hand is to you now, lying there with my sister, breathing. How I adored what we had - that love that only comes your way from your mother. But how I loathed the way the universe worked sometimes, with its abject indifference to our little lives, and its black notions of desolation. Or so it seemed to me as I woke. I'll say bye for now.

Zoe Halloway woke differently to Zen Halloway. As Favola was actually in Earth's orbit directly above her home at that moment, she had a clear vision of Corda's great smiling face as Corda manoeuvred the craft to Angle 79 for a perfect alignment into hyperspace, though she did not know who Corda was. It was, it seemed, a memory. But no, not a memory - because Zoe had no idea whose face it was! The face was… *different,* was all she could conceive of, blinking as she came to in a fading dream. Favola listed away from the Earth *as* Zoe came to, paused, then vanished on a powerful light-trajectory flash which would take it beyond Earth's galaxy and the by now familiar 10-dimensional creatures, who were, of course, the only Type III civilization there - although they would always be able to intercept Favola anywhere in the universe, in an instant.

"Sharp. 19. Angle 82." Peeler Curvature calmly placed commands in Corda's ear, happy and sanguine on a job done well. "It simply never happened to her," he then cryptically remarked, as the craft powered belly-out via its gravity-amplifiers a million-times beyond the speed of light.

"Quite, sir. However, it did happen to us, as has been documented. I am happy that Favola finally returned to Earth - even though it wasn't of its doing…"

"Maybe not, Corda. But Favola has grown from the experience. Look, even now, as we enter hyperspace, she uses the colours and shapes as a creature who communicates in patterns! Behold!" Peeler Curvature turned from the viewing-screen to watch the new shapes on the bridge. Corda also glanced behind at these colours, but soon resumed his position. Yes, *his*. It seemed Corda had also been evolving: he was now - male! Or at least the android equivalent. "Captain, you are perhaps experiencing some poetical input into your thought-processes. The colours of hyperspace look no different to me. I don't see how Favola is communicating in colours, sir." His voice also had deepened.

"Ah, Corda, you wouldn't! You will exist for all time in your current shape and body. I, on the other hand, have only another 200 years or so remaining, sadly - before, who knows! Maybe even us human-species continue after our demise? It's a big thought, my friend." Peeler Curvature stood motionless *in* thought behind Corda, with a firm hand on his shoulder, as Favola zoomed beyond Earth's vast galaxy and across interstellar-space to another distant galaxy. He had not truly noticed the big android's alteration, however. That would come later, when the captain was possibly more relaxed. But, in a powerful juxtaposition to this, the new Type III civilization, whose galaxy they had now instantly entered, had not only been monitoring them since the previous Type IIIs had engendered their inception, but had very different powers and devices with which to ponder the Big Crunch and the new universe beyond. This civilization was a newer species to Earth's; although that didn't make them any less infinite or spectacular…

They dwelled in the harmonies from vibrating

tiny strings, Favola would discover, but that would be all it would discover. This Type III was the Type III to out-Type-III all other Type IIIs - almost…

It seems they initially set the superstrings vibrating in this universe, from surviving the Big Crunch from the last universe, with energies 2 quadrillion times larger than anything that will ever be available on any normal rock-based planet anywhere. *They set the strings vibrating!* Actually *beyond* Planck energy, Zen Halloway was informed. Though, again, as boy with adult comprehension.

And, as with all Type III civilizations who are 10-dimensional in form, these can also move through solid matter as if it wasn't there. For it transpired that all 10-dimensional beings are in communication with the myriad individual minds that we human beings, in death, return to. This was also what Zen was told. In the death-transition, it seems, human beings go back to what they always were: namely, an eternal, large, ethereal consciousness, which, although individual, can merge at will with anything else - including 10-dimensional beings that still mostly exist in the material universe - within dark-matter. Human beings, then, are, in some respects, a Type III civilization already, Zen believed. Or so he mused. In death, he felt, we merge back to the 10-dimensional beings that we already were! Perhaps he hoped this, as well.

Zoe Halloway and her husband Joel were at a

symphony concert in old San Francisco. All was apparently well. Life was good. Just recently she'd been to a time when her grandchildren's children were dying of old age - albeit in another part of the universe - in a craft where X-ray lasers were used to see and work with atoms, as the scientist-species had been doing with the rare alloy. But Brewan, her husband, would never know this, because, in a sense, she hadn't. That is, not on Earth, anyway. And Earth was still where it was at for human beings - it was where 'reality' was. Yet she had been to the future within Favola - and on Earth, a thousand years hence! She had been to another time in space altogether, but with no recall of it!

Miraculously, was an adverb that kept entering her mind, though, relating to the old overseer. One of Zoe Halloway's loves on Earth was new classical music. That is, composers living who wrote serious art-music. She herself had a serious interest in it. And that interest was at the fore now, as she whispered something technical in her husband's ear regarding the, as she perceived it, *miraculous,* music, and the orchestra banged out some soft-grinding dissonant chords that were themselves somehow also harmonic. They smiled knowingly to each other, happy in the sounds - a happy couple - a close bond. Indeed, both of them had a keen interest in music, and, as musicians themselves, often felt that music had a keen interest in them. Music was one of the abiding concepts which had binded Zoe and Brewan together, as Zen knew…

As would be known, Zoe Halloway went on to be the first world-leader of Earth, and would eventually retirc in her late 60s. (Music would again become acutely important to her then). She would also fund her son's (invention?) of the X-ray laser, and the eventuality of actually *seeing* the superstrings which atoms were ultimately constructed of! But for now, Zoe Halloway was the only human being to have taken Earth-music with her to the far side of the holographic universe - inside her brain.

Back aboard Favola, in the silent darkness of musical deep space, (the background noise to space was a constant B-flat, as we now know) while Zoe and her husband moved in the same spacetime on Earth but in an entirely different movement of music and the blue planet's gravitational swing amidst the great sway of its swirling sun, Corda was informed that the new 10-dimensional beings, whose different galaxy they were now in, wished to convey to them that they were welcome in their space, and that everything was already known about Favola. *Everything?*

"The message is, captain, that we harbour no secrets from them." Corda sighed, himself calm with this message; although his burgeoning sexuality had him at a new-found loss, it would be recorded…

The captain and Xenon Ream, on hearing this

information, insisted on knowing who was communicating with them. For the communication was being done in intricate symbols, which Favola simultaneaously received translations for. The intelligence, again, was of a form beyond Favola's comprehension. As with the 28-dimensional calculations, the symbols were totally unknown. Whatever minds caused their inception were, as before, beyond anything Favola had encountered thus far.

All motion-drives were at a standstill, as the great craft hung inert in an infinite void…

Printed in Great Britain
by Amazon

15538561R00119